Welcome

Happy Reading 🙂

Jana Philips   Sic' Em !

POWER LIES

By J. L. Phillips

Published by Phillips Publishing.
www.JanaLairdPhillips.com

In Association with:
Elite Online Publishing
63 East 11400 South, #230
Sandy, UT 84070
EliteOnlinePublishing.com

Printed in the United States of America.

ISBN: 978-1707875160

For my angel, Dave.

For Woody.

Thanks to my editor, Jessica Schwend

Thanks to my publisher, Elite Online Publishing

CHAPTER ONE

Slap! Harry Brown woke, cheek burning. A bearded stranger stood over him.

He tried to get out of the recliner, but was pushed down, his robe askew.

"Sit down and stay put," the intruder said, inches from Harry's face. He looked vaguely familiar.

"What do you want?"

"You betrayed us."

"Who are you?"

Only moments earlier, Harry had been watching the Orioles lose to the Red Sox, his cat, Raven, asleep on a pile of once-clean clothes. Just over the stranger's shoulder, his grungy cable box glowed 10:30 p.m.

At least Sarah isn't here. No telling what this guy would do to her.

The intruder clamped Harry's chin with a single strong hand, forcing their eyes to meet.

"The woman that was here today. What did you tell her?"

"What woman?"

Harry took a deep breath and coughed up greenish mucus. The man's damp trench coat smelled like sweat and scotch. A bead of water fell from the lapel to Harry's naked knee.

"Sterling, what'd she want?"

The intruder's words slurred, and spit sprayed onto Harry's face.

"They sent you? I promise, I never revealed the secret. Please, I'm a sick man." Harry coughed again.

"I saw you talk to her." He pulled on leather gloves.

Isn't it a little late for that? Oh wait, unless…

The intruder punched him in the face, hard. Harry shielded his now bleeding cheek with shaking hands.

"Stop, please, stop. Yes, I did talk to her, but I didn't divulge anything. I've always been loyal to the industry. Please, I need to take my pills."

The man didn't budge.

"Look at me, I'm dying."

The man crushed Harry's shoulders with a vise-like grip.

"Tell me what I want to know, or you can die in the next five minutes."

Oh no. I need a weapon. Anything.

Harry pushed his robe aside, let his bladder loose, and sprayed urine in the man's face.

"You son of a bitch!" The intruder jumped back spitting and rubbing his eyes, tripped over an ottoman and hit the brick fireplace hard.

Harry bolted from the recliner, old joints creaking, and ran for the kitchen door.

Dazed, the intruder stumbled and grabbed the mantle to steady himself. Harry's family pictures and snow globe collection tumbled to the floor, shattering. The man rubbed the back of his head and saw Harry in the kitchen fumbling with door locks.

"You're going to regret that."

Harry abandoned the locks and grabbed a paring knife next to a half-peeled, slimy apple.

The intruder charged him.

Knife in hand, Harry lunged at the man, who swerved, avoiding the blade. Harry focused on the front door and tried to channel all remaining energy into his legs.

The intruder grabbed Harry by the neck.

Harry flailed, stabbing the knife behind him. The man caught his wrist and bent it backwards, until something popped, and Harry lost feeling, falling to his knees.

This is it. I'm sorry Sarah.

Harry wheezed.

"Forget what you said to the woman. Give me your notes and this will end."

The man kicked Harry and his face hit the cold linoleum. At that very moment, a piercing yowl echoed through the room and Raven pounced panther-like on the man, clawing his cheeks and forehead. The intruder yelled, swiping at the cat.

"Get off me, you mangy animal."

The man clawed back at the cat and threw it across the kitchen. The cat landed on all fours with a screech and streaked out of the room.

"No more bullshit, Harry."

4

The man dragged Harry off the floor and dumped him in the recliner, his thin, worn, body exposed.

I have no power over this guy, except…

"You can kill me, but the truth will come out."

The man punched Harry in the face. His head fell forward, nodding like a bobble head doll.

The man seized the lamp from the end table next to the recliner, and the shade tumbled to the floor. He ripped the electrical cord from the base and tossed the lamp aside. He stretched the cord taut, wrapped it around Harry's neck, and squeezed tight.

A blackness came over Harry and he saw Sarah.

"Traitor" the intruder said.

****

The man dropped the lamp's power cord and stared into Harry's frozen eyes.

So, this is what it feels like to kill someone. My temper got the better of me. I must protect the industry. I just wanted his damn notes, and for him to keep his mouth shut. Well, he won't talk now. Serves him right for peeing in my face. Ugh, something smells horrible. Probably this pigsty.

He ran his gloved hand through his hair, wiped the sweat off his brow, and walked to the back of the house to begin his search. A single bulb lit the dark and musty hallway. He could barely fit into the back room, filled to the ceiling with newspapers, magazines, and file cabinets.

He choked on dust while he tossed the room. Finding nothing of value, he moved on to the bedroom, living room, and kitchen, tearing each apart.

Damn it. No notes. Unless, he gave them to Sterling. She'll pay for this. I can't let her publish that information.

He left the house and walked onto the dark front porch; the humidity overwhelming. Tried to take a deep breath then vomited into a holly bush. He removed his gloves and wiped his mouth.

Will this heat ever end? The Grid can't take much more.

For the first time in years, he longed for a cigarette. To light one, watch the fire catch hold of the tobacco, and take a long, slow drag.

He yanked a flask from his trench coat pocket and took a swig. The smooth, dark liquid burned his throat. A good scotch, like a good lover, made him want more.

The cat scratches stung, and blood trickled down his face. He ran a handkerchief over the wounds.

Damn pussy. Both of 'em.

He looked over what was once a decent middle-class white neighborhood, with well-kept yards, maintained houses, and content children. Now the dilapidated houses hid shady characters. He could not imagine why Harry stayed here.

A large bolt of lightning attacked the nearby Maryland Power substation. Sparks traveled in every direction off the towers. Within three seconds he heard the boom of thunder, and his heart skipped a beat.

Damn close. The Maryland Power linemen'll be busy tonight.

Calmer now, he walked down the crumbling neighborhood sidewalk as steaming drizzle turned into steady rain. He turned up the collar of his coat and tucked his head down.

A few blocks from Harry's house, he used a rundown gas station pay phone to call a cab. He took another swig from his flask and called the private line.

"Hey, it's me. I need to see you tonight. Yeah, I know what time it is. There's something you need to know. No, I can't go into it on the phone. Meet me at the Center Café. Yeah, that's the one.

You'll be proud."

CHAPTER TWO

The balcony door blew shut startling the young woman as she zipped up her black silk cocktail dress. Strong winds signaled oncoming storms. Tall and slender, Sterling Barrington, was getting ready for a date with Congressman Trevor Reese. She slipped on red leather heels and clicked across the dark wood floor, reopening the door. Lightning illuminated the skies. The enemy of power lines.

Across from her apartment building, twilight settled over the glistening headstones of Arlington Cemetery. She heard Taps being played at the Iwo Jima Memorial nearby.

Sterling never tired of these sights and sounds. It reminded her that she wasn't alone in tragically losing a loved one. A young boy's smile flashed through her mind. She smoothed her long red hair and wiped tears away from her blue eyes.

While touching up her makeup, Sterling recalled how disappointing her trip to Baltimore had been. She wanted Harry Brown to have all the answers about electromagnetic fields (also known as EMFs), their tie to cancer, and the denial of said tie by the electric industry. Her industry. She needed the truth.

****

Sterling left her old life and job at the Atlanta Light Company in 2005, known commonly as ALC, to become the Vice President of Public Relations, for the prestigious Franklin Energy Institute in Washington, D.C known simply as The Franklin. Made up of industry experts, this trade association was founded to optimize power grid efficiency.

After deregulation, in the late 1990's, the 47 lower contiguous states, with the exception of Texas, were connected by a national electric grid. Power could be "wheeled" or sold across the country. A person in Georgia could buy power from a provider in Illinois.

The former monopolistic electric utilities were forced to compete for customers for the first time. Competition and marketing were foreign to this industry, which is why the industry boomed when new provider companies started advertising power discounts across the country. Families sat down to dinner, only to be interrupted with annoying phone calls from these companies, offering them discounts, promotions, even airline miles, to switch from their old electric provider to a new provider. This is how Sterling hit The Franklin's talent radar.

Her professional reputation as an image "fixer" and profit lifter in the electric industry gained her national recognition and caught the ear of Walker Nelson, The Franklin's Director of Marketing.

In her interview, Walker asked if she could, "Launch a PR campaign to promote the passage of a new energy bill that would allow more power lines, transmission towers, and substations to be built across the country. According to Walker, "The Institute needed the bill passed because more power lines meant no more blackouts, like the one in August 2003, and happier customers."

Sterling's campaign would also have to defend The Franklin's electric company members from the radical environmental groups who threatened their credibility. These groups claimed EMFs emitted by power lines caused illnesses like cancer due to Electrohypersensitivity (EHS).

Walker made it clear to her and everyone within earshot that power lines were safe, and the environmental groups were "anti-establishment, tree-hugging wackos who blamed the industry on all bad things happening in the world."

****

Sterling put down her makeup brush and stared at the clock ticking beside her jewelry box. She didn't feel like going out tonight with Trevor, but he was probably already being chauffeured over. After absentmindedly selecting a silver purse from her closet, Sterling bumped a few books off her nightstand. A newspaper clipping fell out of one and a name caught her eye. Harry Brown.

****

After starting her job at The Franklin, Sterling researched EMFs in the company library. She discovered that two men were considered EMF subject matter experts: Walker and Harry Brown.

Per the file, Harry worked as an electrical engineer at the Department of Energy (DOE) for 41 years. His research documents stated that EMFs did not cause cancer and was quoted in multiple press releases saying as much. However, Harry's contributions to industry PR stopped abruptly in 1999 when, according to a news clipping, "he quit his job after the mysterious death of wife Sarah."

Sterling needed to speak with him.

The DOE gave her Harry's phone number, and she called him to request a meeting. He hung up on her. She called back several times to no avail, then, sent him a certified letter. No response. She'd have to confront him.

Not a soul at The Franklin knew Sterling was trying to contact Harry. She left work and hailed a cab to Union Station.

Entering the station always took Sterling's breath away. At its opening in 1908, the building held the title of the world's largest train station. This gateway had long been hailed the greatest example of the Beaux Arts style. The architect, Daniel Burnham, famed for the 1893 Chicago World's Fair, designed the building to be monumental.

Beneath the 22-karat gold-leaf dome, homeless people begged and sought shelter. A young woman in a tattered, sour smelling dress held out her hand to Sterling while shielding a small child behind her. Sterling gave her a twenty-dollar bill.

It could always be worse.

With tickets purchased, she headed to the Baltimore Express track. While waiting her turn to go through security, she glimpsed a familiar face across the hall.

Sandy? Is that Sandy?

She whirled around to get a better look, shouting "Sandy", and bumped into the man behind her.

"Excuse me." Sterling said.

He gave her a dirty look, muttered something about damned women, and turned away. She searched the throng for her co-worker. The hall bulged with businesspeople in suits, mothers with children, teenagers with backpacks, tourists toting suitcases, but no Sandy. She shrugged off the sighting and moved ahead in line.

On board the train, Sterling claimed a seat in the front car and pulled out her laptop to review her presentation notes for The Franklin Board of Directors meeting.

The humming wheels and whizzing scenery made it difficult to concentrate. The hour-long train trip took her from the expensive Capitol Hill residences to the lower income, high crime areas of Baltimore. These deteriorating neighborhoods so close to the world's power capitol shocked Sterling.

Despite the distracting scenery, Sandy popped back into her head. She knew it was her colleague, Sandford Matthews, but why did he ignore her and then disappear?

Did Sandy follow me?

From her first day at The Franklin, Sandy lurked around with one excuse or another for being near her. His constant presence and refusal to accept romantic invitations unnerved her. She didn't trust him and knew he fed office gossip to Walker.

Sterling returned to her presentation notes until the loudspeaker interrupted, announcing "Next Stop, Baltimore."

She stood up, straightened her suit and exited in search of a taxi.

"869 Vine Street, please" she said. Her Southern accent resonated in the backseat of the yellow cab.

The driver, an older man with a narrow face pushed his cap up and stared at her with dark eyes.

"Lady, that's not a good part of town. You sure that's the right address?"

"Yes, that's the address."

"OK, rough area for the likes of you, but whatever you say."

The weather was dreary, with patchy fog and rain rolling across the cab's hood. This did not ease Sterling's anxiety about meeting Harry.

Would he talk to her? What did he really know about EMFs? Why did he leave the DOE so suddenly?

"I'm Angelo. So, why's a fancy piece like you going to a shady part of town?" He turned down his dispatch radio.

"Business."

"Not very chatty, are you?"

They drove along in silence until he took a sharp right onto a residential street.

"Is this a shortcut?"

"No, I want to show you something."

"I'm not paying you for a tour."

Sterling pulled out her cell phone, poised to call for help.

"Edgar's house. Have you seen it before?"

"Edgar?

"Yeah, Mr. Poe's home. It's a museum now. Want me to stop? I've been lots of times. I can show you around." Angelo smiled at her in the rearview mirror.

"Not today. I've got to get to my meeting."

"Suit yourself." He grunted and hunched over the steering wheel.

How much further?

Angelo turned down another street and pulled in front of a rundown one-story cottage.

"Here you go, 869 Vine."

Sterling looked out the rain-streaked window at a house haunted by lifelessness. Once white and now a musty gray, she spied a rusted weathervane on the roof and lopsided curtains inside.

"You're sure this is the right address?"

"Only one in Baltimore, that'll be…"

"Thanks. Here's a fifty. Twenty more if you wait for me. It shouldn't take long." Sterling smiled, pushed the bill through the divider window and waved it at Angelo's face.

"Sure, why not."

She started up the sinking sidewalk towards the house and noticed a rickety garage beside the house, sagging doors closed with no sign of cars. The cracked doorbell button didn't look safe, so she knocked loudly.

She waited, business card at the ready.

I hope he's home.

"Mr. Brown? Harry? Anyone there?"

"Hold your horses, I'm coming." Said a weak male voice from inside. The door opened, and a frail man looked Sterling up and down, then asked "What're you selling?"

"Mr. Brown, I'm Sterling Barrington, from The Franklin. It's imperative I speak with you about EMFs."

"You? I don't have anything to say."

Harry opened the screen door, took a tentative step on to the porch, and scanned the street.

"I came alone. Please, I need your help. You're a revered expert on EMFs, but you left the DOE so suddenly. Why?"

A slender black cat slithered out of the narrow space between Harry and the door, rubbing against Sterling's legs, purring.

"Raven, get back in here. Lady, leave me alone. I'm dying."

"Please, help me. It's personal."

"No, I can't help anyone."

Harry wheezed, shooed the cat inside and started to close the door, but Sterling pushed her business card into his bony hand.

"You can trust me. If you change your mind, call."

He took the card and closed the door.

She stood on the porch for a moment.

Progress.

"You done?" Angelo said as she slid back into the cab. Air conditioner hit her face.

It smelled musty. Like Harry.

"Back to the station, Angelo."

CHAPTER THREE

"Last call for the Philadelphia Express. Final boarding on track 29," the public address system blared in Union Station. Station visitors walked by the Center Café, a round double-decked bar in the middle of the lobby, oblivious to the lone man on the upper deck glaring down at them. Sandy Matthews gulped his second scotch and checked the time on his Rolex.

When will he get here?

Sweat beaded on his forehead so he took off his Burberry trench coat and laid it over a chairback. One of his leather gloves fell to the floor. The sweating got worse. He groaned and leaned down to retrieve it, damp salt and pepper hair falling over his eyes.

Harry had to die.

Sandy's chest tightened. He inhaled and exhaled deeply in an attempt to calm his nerves. He looked older than 35 thanks to the worry lines and stubborn greys. Today he felt 65.

God, I hope I don't have a heart attack.

Harry's demise wasn't the only traumatic event he'd experienced lately. Last week, his wife of eight years, Helene, left him for another man. She called Sandy a fag and told him he'd never been man enough for her.

Furious at her accusation, he hit her across the face. Helene pressed charges and he landed in jail overnight for domestic abuse. He got out on bond and would be in court next month.

He shivered. Helene had spoken the truth. Sandy had been suppressing his homosexual lust since he was 14. He preferred sex with men and hated himself for it.

Sandy's father, a steely lineman for Mass Electric, would have disowned him if he knew the secret. In an effort to please him, Sandy worked in Mass Electric's customer service department after college graduation. He focused on his work, not sex.

He met Helene at a friend's out-of-town wedding. She seemed like the perfect woman; a sophisticated, successful investment banker seven years his senior. They consumed a large amount of alcohol at the reception and went back to Sandy's hotel room.

When he didn't get an erection, Helene took control of the situation. She rolled him over, sat on top of him, and pleased herself. Afterwards, she criticized his lack of performance, and told him she would make him a better lover. Her severe critique was shattering to his already suppressed ego.

A week later Helene called and said she wanted to start over. He decided to give her another chance. Maybe he could be happy with a woman. They dated and married a year later. She tutored him in the ways of sex and business.

Thanks to his tutor's success, Sandy met Walker through networking at electric industry meetings. They struck up a friendship, and Walker hired him for a prestigious job at The Franklin. Helene, thrilled with his new high-profile position, transferred her job to DC. For the first time, he felt content.

Two years later, jilted and depressed, Sandy went to bars with Walker several times a week to fill the void. He appreciated Walker as a mentor and friend. He'd do anything for the man. Today, he proved his loyalty.

Sometimes, proud-to-be-gay Bob Turner, The Franklin's head of accounting joined them. Although Sandy had chemistry with Bob, he refused to acknowledge it. When Sterling started at The Franklin, he openly admired her figure and immediately asked her out.

I'll seduce Sterling to make Helene jealous.

Sterling rebuffed his first and subsequent attempts to date

her, and after her actions today,

he loathed her.

She will pay.

CHAPTER FOUR

Sterling snapped the clasp on her pearls, a sweet 16 gift from Mother and Father, then fastened the last button on her silk jacket. Her phone rang. The concierge told her Congressman Reese had arrived.

A few minutes later, there was a knock at Sterling's door.

"Hello, beautiful. These are for you." Reese said as he walked into her apartment with a bouquet of stargazer lilies.

"They're lovely. Let me put them in water and we can go." Sterling gently kissed his lips and patted the lapels of his navy blazer.

Trevor Reese, freshman congressman also from Atlanta, former collegiate track star and Environmental Protection Agency (EPA) legal counsel, was now a member of the joint House/Senate Energy committee. His ebony skin and athletic build caught Sterling's eye the first time she saw him at a fundraising dinner.

Downstairs his midnight blue Lincoln Town Car, with congressional plates, waited. His driver, Tom Whitaker, a silver-haired man in his sixties, opened the door.

"Since you're still new to D.C., I'm taking you to some of my favorite spots tonight."

Their first stop; the rooftop bar at the Hotel Washington. A popular, intimate watering hole in the District, enclosed in the cool months and open in the warmer months, with an exceptional view of the White House, Treasury Department and Washington monument.

"Welcome, Congressman. What can I get you two tonight?" the attentive waiter said.

"Hello, Jim. We'll have my favorite Pinot Noir and the baked brie. Thanks."

They watched the presidential motorcade leave the White House. Trevor took her hand in his.

"I wonder where the President's dining tonight?" Sterling said.

"You told me you had a big meeting. Did it go well?"

"Well, not as good as I hoped. Let's not talk about that right now."

She pulled her hand out of his and sat back as the waiter approached.

"Here you go, Congressman." Jim said.

"Thanks, Jim" Trevor said.

The waiter poured the wine, set the bottle on the table, and walked away.

"Sterling, what's wrong?"

"I received another one of those anonymous letters today. The most disturbing one, so far."

She pulled the letter from her purse.

"I'm worried these groups will come after you. Let me investigate EMFs. That's why I'm on the Energy Committee."

"Trevor, we haven't dated very long, but you should know by now, once I'm determined to find a solution to a problem, I won't give up."

"I know, you have that Southern female determination. With a Mother and four sisters, I'm very familiar with it. Tell me what they sent this time."

"An article about a 1996 class action suit in Houston involving ten families with sick children who sued the local electric company, Houston Electric, and the Electric Research Institute (ERI), the research arm of the electric industry. The Franklin works with ERI on joint projects all the time. Trevor, these families met because their children were in the same hospital, being treated for cancer and

leukemia. I couldn't help but think of my nephew Chris."

"I'm not familiar with this case. When I worked at the EPA, I

worked on water cases. It might have been settled out of court. Who

represented the families?"

"Joe Johnson. Do you know him?"

"Yes. He won one of the largest cases ever in the energy

industry, back in the 1980s."

"The article stated the lawsuit charged the defendants with two

counts: conspiracy and negatively affecting the families' property

values. The plaintiffs believed Houston Electric and ERI hid and

discredited data regarding EMFs emitted from power lines that could

cause cancer in children."

"Go on."

"Johnson blamed the utility for affecting the families' property

values. His fourteen-point list of accusations included that EMFs were

proven cancer risks and that the two electric entities conspired to

falsify and conceal facts, which proved EMFs cause cancer. Johnson

claimed the magnetic fields in question were stronger than the levels

proven to cause childhood cancer. He asserted the illnesses and deaths could have been prevented by the defendants because Houston

Electric had the knowledge and technology available to insulate the

public from the magnetic field exposure danger. He also stated that

Houston Electric conducted their operations in a reckless and unsafe

manner to avoid extra expenses associated with safely conducting

operations."

"Johnson must have scared Houston Electric shitless."

"There's more. Houston Electric chose not to publicize their

prudent avoidance stance. Johnson claimed prudent avoidance was

considered a guide for interactions with electricity. I did some

research and found out prudent avoidance meant moving beds away

from high EMF sites, disposing of electric blankets and alarm clocks,

and standing as far away as possible from microwave ovens. Houston

Electric stated they did not adhere to this philosophy because they

wanted to wait for an industry consensus regarding the hazards of

EMFs."

"Does The Franklin promote prudent avoidance to their utility

members?"

"No. The Franklin hasn't publicized any information on

EMFs. From my research on EMFs, I learned when you plug in an appliance, an electric field exists, and a magnetic field exists when the appliance is operating. So, power lines do in fact emit electromagnetic fields. I started working at The Franklin to defend the industry against crazy extremists who claim power lines cause cancer. Now, I don't know what to believe."

"That's why I'm trying to learn about EMFs before I vote on the proposed Energy Bill. And, what do you know, look who's making yet another entrance."

Sterling turned her head toward the doorway where one of the most powerful men in Washington, Senator Anthony Morelli stood. He paused for a moment to ensure everyone saw him. The senior Senator from New York, with his six-foot four-inch frame, wide shoulders and skyscraper ego, filled the small rooftop bar. As Chairman of the Joint Energy Committee, he benefitted most if the Energy Bill was passed. After the Blackout in August 2003 that scourged the Northeast, he never wanted his constituents to experience such a catastrophe again.

Sterling watched Morelli survey the room and advance on the most buzz-worthy target.

"Congressman, how are you?" the Senator said when he walked to their table.

Trevor stood up and shook the man's hand.

"Hello, Senator. Nice to see you."

"Ms. Barrington, you look lovely this evening. I didn't know you two were friends." He leaned over and kissed Sterling on the cheek.

"Senator, thank you. It's a pleasure."

"Reese, we need to get together to discuss your vote. I'll be in touch."

"I'm still undecided."

"Yes, well, we can always change that, Congressman. Have a nice evening, Ms. Barrington."

"Good night, Senator." Trevor said.

The Senator walked away to greet other patrons. Trevor turned back to Sterling.

"He wants me to vote for the Energy Bill. He believes, as does The Franklin, that more power lines mean less chance of a blackout. But more power lines mean more EMFs."

"Yes, more power lines, do mean less chance of a blackout. I know all about the 2003 blackout. I was attending an industry seminar in New York City when it hit. That's where I met Walker. At first, we all presumed it was an act of terrorism. Everyone tried to use their cell phones and Blackberries, but they wouldn't work. Fifty million people survived without power, transportation, or air conditioning for hours. August in the Big Apple is hot. In fact, the blackout and Walker's drunken rants during said event, made me believe more power lines were needed if we're to prevent this from happening again. Walker considers himself an expert on EMFs and he let everyone know it. Our grid system should've worked, and it didn't that time."

"What caused the blackout?"

"A domino effect with the power lines. The U.S. and Canada connect at 37 points so the two countries can trade power to prevent problems. When one U.S. utility has a shortage, they buy power from a neighboring utility. It turned out the U.S. network used an old transmission grid of underground and overhead power lines from the 1950's. Walker and my peers said, 'I told you so'. They believed there had been too little investment in the transmission grid and the existing grid became too complex for its age. They believed deregulation ruined the industry by breaking up utilities and separating transmission businesses from the generators that produce electricity. Now, the independent operators dominate the industry in a market-driven system, which, some of my peers believe, created a broken link between generation planning and transmission planning."

"I see their point, but all deregulations take time to sort out. The electric industry needed to be deregulated; some of those utilities were becoming too big."

"I can't agree with you, yet. But I know I can't work for an industry that lied, or perhaps killed innocent people. Let's not talk about work anymore. I want to enjoy the evening with you."

"Ready for our next stop?"

Alone, inside the elevator, Trevor pulled Sterling to him and kissed her. Outside the Hotel Washington, he put his arm around her waist as they walked around the corner of 16th street and entered the Willard Hotel lobby.

"I wanted you to see the Willard because it's a political landmark in DC. This is THE power lunch location. In fact, the term lobbyist came from the deals politicians made in this lobby. Look up at the ceiling, Sterling. When the Willard renovated in the 1980's, they painted the ceiling with all 50 states' seals."

"Magnificent. The marble floors, Corinthian columns and oriental carpets."

"Come on, let's eat on to The Occidental."

One of the oldest and historical restaurants in the District, The Occidental, sat next door to the Willard. Sterling gazed at the walls filled with photographs of past and present Hill members and DC luminaries.

"If only those photos could talk," Sterling said.

They settled into a high-walled banquette and the waiter took their order.

"I know you're doing the best you can regarding EMFs. I'm glad you're here and that we met."

"So, am I. But I will find out the truth."

After dinner, Trevor's car and driver waited outside the restaurant with chilled champagne and strawberries.

"A final surprise for the evening, a tour of the monuments before the rain comes again."

****

"Good morning, sleepyhead" Trevor said. He moved her hair away from her face and kissed her cheek.

"Um, good morning. What time is it?"

"It's 4:00 am. I have a 7:00 am breakfast meeting, and if I want to get my run in, I need to leave now."

"Ok, talk to you later. Thanks again for last night."

Sterling pulled the covers up to her chin and looked forward to more sleep before her 6:00 AM alarm. As she drifted off, the buzz of her mobile phone jolted her awake. She groaned and grabbed the phone from her nightstand. The clock glowed 4:15 am.

"Trevor, did you forget something?"

"St-Sterling?"

"Hello, who is it? I can't hear you, please speak up."

"It's, it's Blythe, I need your help."

Sterling sat up in bed.

"Blythe? What's wrong?"

"I'm in trouble, can you meet me?"

"Of course, I'll help you. Where are you?"

"I'm in Baltimore."

"Give me the address. At this hour I can be there in 45 minutes, maybe less, if I don't see any police."

"I don't need any cops. I'm at 869 Vine Street."

"Did you say 869 Vine? What are you doing at Harry Brown's house?"

"Forget it. I thought I could trust you."

"No, wait, don't hang up. It's just that, never mind. I'm leaving in five minutes. Don't go anywhere. I'll be there. Blythe, what are you doing with Harry?

"Harry's dead."

CHAPTER FIVE

Sandy saw his boss march up the café steps and attempted to clear his head. Walker pointed to the dried blood on Sandy's ear.

"What the hell happened to you?"

Despite decades in America, Walker's British accent still surfaced, especially in stressful situations. Probably a Paul Newman lookalike in his younger years, Walker's once-blonde hair was now ashy, and his blue eyes were lifeless. The bulldog wreaked of nicotine and his wrinkled shirt puckered over a well-earned paunch.

"This vodka is yours. You'll need it after I tell you...hey, I thought you quit." Sandy motioned to the cigarette in Walker's hand.

"Shut up. What the fuck happened tonight?"

"Harry Brown died."

"How the hell would you know?"

"Because I killed him."

"Holy Shit. What did the old bastard do to you?"

"It's what he did to us, to the industry. The other day I saw Sterling in The Franklin library doing research for her PR campaign.

At first, I didn't think much of it, but then I overheard her talking on the phone to Harry Brown."

"Go on."

"I thought, why does she need to talk to him? So, when she left the office today, I followed her. She went to see Harry in Baltimore." Sandy took a large swig of his scotch. "I hid across the street while the two of them stood on the porch and talked. I couldn't hear anything, but something went down."

"Will Mr. Greg Wagner please meet his party at the information booth?" The P.A. system announced. Sandy looked around the Union Station lobby where a few late-night travelers roamed.

"I waited until dark and confronted Harry."

Walker's face paled. He took a sharp breath, jammed a half-finished cigarette into a nearby ashtray and gulped vodka, ice sloshing when the glass hit the table.

"What'd he tell you?"

"He said Sterling knew nothing. I didn't believe him, so Harry won't be telling anyone, anything, anymore. I remembered the night you confided in me about the industry's biggest cover-up. Now, Walker, the loose lips have been sealed and your secret is safe."

"Well done, Sandy. What a weak son of a bitch Harry was. I bet he did tell that saucy Sterling everything. Hey, honey, another round here." Walker said to the waitress who hovered near the table. "Did Harry do that to your ear?" Walker lit another cigarette and blew the smoke over the bar's railing.

"No, Harry's cat did. Forget that, we need to talk about what to do with that nosy bitch. I tore his house apart looking for you know what but came up with nothing. He must've given his notes to her."

"Sterling has Harry's notes? Shit. We've got to keep this information away from the public. It could ruin the industry and our careers." Walker considered, just for a second, where his set of notes lived.

"Should I shut her up like I did Harry?"

"That cunt. Who does she think she is? Well, she isn't about to save the world. She didn't see you, right?

"No, sir."

"Good. Let's see how she acts at work and catch up tomorrow. Go get some rest and bandage that ear."

CHAPTER SIX

Sterling programmed Harry's home address into her car's GPS, tightly clutching the wheel as she sped to Baltimore.

Harry's dead? Was he silenced by someone? Why is Blythe at Harry's?

Forty minutes later, brain pounding with questions, she pulled her Lexus into Harry's driveway; the headlights eerily lit the cracked, discolored paint on the derelict house. Sterling snapped off her high beams, popped out of the car and hurriedly shut the door. Smack, smack, smack. The door had slammed shut, echoing down the street and shattering the early morning silence.

Damn.

After a few cautious steps, her eyes adjusted to the darkness. There were streetlights, but none with working bulbs. The grass squished beneath her feet as she approached the front door and sweat trickled between her breasts.

Thankfully, there was a porch light that illuminated the steps, poorly due to the cobwebs and mildew covering it, but helpful all the same. She pushed the unlocked front door aside and stepped into the house nervously calling, "Blythe, it's me." Sterling's voice cracked

when she saw Harry's exposed body slumped in a recliner. She took a

step closer and saw the electrical cord wrapped around his neck. His

face was bruised and bloated, eyes frozen in fear, and thin hair matted

with sweat.

Who did this?

"Don't touch him!" Blythe said.

Sterling jumped back from the body and turned to see Blythe

stride out of the kitchen with a duffel bag over her right shoulder,

gold locket swinging from side to side around her neck.

Sterling went over and hugged her. Blythe stood rigid at first,

then relaxed and gingerly returned the embrace.

Blythe still smelled of the same perfume; the one she'd worn

since high school.

"Are you ok? I've been worried about you. I'm sorry I left

you alone in Atlanta."

Blythe withdrew from Sterling's arms and walked over to look

at Harry's body.

"I'll be fine. Did you touch the body?"

"No. Blythe, why are you here?"

"I'm here, for SAFEPOWER. I had an appointment with Harry."

"An appointment? This early?"

"Yes. Yesterday, Harry called SAFEPOWER. Carter didn't believe him at first. But he researched him on the web and read his bio."

"Carter? Who's Carter?"

"Carter Thompson, our leader, my leader, SAFEPOWER's leader."

"Ok. Go on, about Harry's call.

"Anyway, Carter called Harry back. Harry told him the electric industry, his industry, and your industry, lied. He said he knew the truth. He said the murders had to stop. He wanted to give us his documents on EMFs, so SAFEPOWER could get the truth out to the public before the Energy bill went to vote. He said the Energy Bill must not pass so that no more power lines could be built. He'd heard me on the news conference and wanted to give me the evidence to prove the EMFs killed my son, his wife, and himself. He told me to be here at 4:00 am. So, I came, alone. This is how I found him. Achoo!"

"He said his wife died because of EMFs?"

"Did you see that huge substation a block away? He said that substation caused their cancers."

"Yes, I saw it. Blythe, listen to me. Ever since you claimed Chris died because of EMFs, I've searched for the truth about power lines and cancer. I must know if my industry concealed the truth. I came to see Harry early yesterday to ask him what he knew. But he wouldn't speak with me. So, just to be clear, he was dead when you arrived?"

"Look, I didn't kill him if that's what you're getting at. You're not listening to me. He wanted to help us." Blythe pulled a tissue from her pocket and blew her nose.

"I'm sorry. I get it now."

"Achoo."

"Are you sick?"

"No, it's this house. I'm allergic to the mold and dust in here."

Sterling looked around realizing that someone had torn the house apart, making the decay airborne. "Whoever killed Harry must have been looking for his notes. At least you didn't walk in on the killer."

"That's true. I didn't know what to do when I found Harry this way."

"I'm glad you called me. What can I do to help?" Sterling reached over and squeezed Blythe's hand. "Shall we start by calling the police?"

"No. No police. I can't have the police here. They won't believe me. I can't let SAFEPOWER get negative publicity. They're my family now," she said while squeezing her locket.

"Blythe, I'm your family, not that radical group. You called me. Now, we're going to do the right thing. We have to report this to the police. I'll stay with you. It'll be fine."

"I told you NO. I won't stay. I've, I've got to take care of something later. I wanted to give you another chance, but I must get back to SAFEPOWER. I'll be missed."

"Okay, I'll handle this. I'll stay and talk to the police. They'll never know you were here."

"You'd do that for me?"

"I'm your sister. I love you."

Blythe headed for the front door, stopped and turned back toward Sterling.

"Thanks, Sterling."

"Blythe, wait. Where're you going? I didn't see a car outside."

"I parked a few blocks away and walked here."

"How can I get in touch with you? Please, don't do anything you'll regret."

"I'll be fine. I'll be with my SAFEPOWER family. I'll call you later, I promise."

Blythe gave Sterling a small smile and shut the door. Alone with Harry, Sterling shook her head. "You knew the truth Harry, and it got you killed."

CHAPTER SEVEN

The rain came down in sheets outside Union Station. Walker held a newspaper over his head as he got in a cab.

"5615 Woodley Park Boulevard" he told the cab driver, lighting a cigarette and rolling down a window.

Shit. Shit. Shit. What a fucking mess.

His marriage, his health, and now he had to worry about his job.

I hired Sterling to save my career, not ruin it.

It rained the day he hired Sterling, a bad omen. Her beauty mesmerized him at an industry conference in New York, plus she had smarts. Why did she have to be moral?

Her public relations work at the Atlanta Light Company completely turned the business around. Her positive marketing plan brought back customers from the new, unregulated competitors. Walker needed a miracle worker to save his industry from all the naysayers and get the public to support the passing of the Energy Bill.

"Walker, that woman's here for the interview," Toni, his assistant, said.

"What interview? What the fuck are you talking about?"

"It's ok, Walker, honey, I know your memory is on the fritz. Your interview's with Sterling Barrington, for the PR job. Here's her resumé. You met her in New York during the Blackout." She patted his hand.

Toni knew Walker inside out and outside in. Although their tryst ended years ago, she still loved him.

"Oh, yeah, give me a minute. I'll meet her in the conference room. What's your first impression of her?"

"She's prompt, professional, with a charming Southern accent."

Walker took her hand in his and squeezed. "Thanks, Toni."

"Sure thing, honey. Take your time; I'll give her a cup of coffee. And don't worry, sugar, your secret's safe with me." She straightened her short, tight skirt and left his office.

Shit. I don't remember this appointment. Yesterday, I forgot where I left my keys, and Eileen let me in the house. What next? I do remember Toni, though. Maybe once more for old time's sake.

He met with Sterling and hired her that day. She would be his savior and fend off the crazy environmental groups that made his life a living hell, then get the Energy Bill passed.

How did he misread her? Her beauty clouded his judgment.

He blew smoke out the window, pulled out his cell phone, and punched in the private number of one of the power brokers in Washington.

"Who the hell's this?" Senator Morelli said.

"Tony, it's Walker, we have a problem. We need to meet. It can't wait."

"It better be important to interrupt me now. What is it?" The Senator sat up in his four-poster bed in the Watergate Apartments.

"Which blonde intern are you screwing tonight, Tony?"

"Fuck you, Walker. What's the problem?

"I'll tell you when I see you. Where do you want to meet?"

"The diner on Wisconsin. Georgetown Café. I'll be there in 45 minutes."

"Right. See you there."

Walker flicked his cigarette butt out the window. If only he could get rid of Sterling so easily.

"Change of plans, take me to the Georgetown Café on Wisconsin." Walker told the cab driver. His cell phone rang and broke the silence. He looked at the caller ID, his wife, Eileen.

"Yeah, what do you want? I know it's late. I told you I had to take care of business. I'll be home when I get home." He slammed the phone closed.

Nag, nag, nag, for the last 15 years. Clingy bitch. She still thinks she's better than me. She got what she wanted, marriage, two brats, shit. I've got my own problems to handle. She can go to hell.

CHAPTER EIGHT

After her sister's departure, Sterling walked through the house and found every room trashed, papers strewn around, drawers opened, closets emptied. Her watch showed 5:45 am. It would be sunrise soon. She would wait until 8:00 a.m. to call the police. She needed time to think about what and how much to divulge. Her PR experience would definitely be useful.

Her parent's death changed the course of her life. They were driving back to Atlanta after visiting her at Vanderbilt University when an out-of-control 18-wheeler broadsided their car. They died at the scene.

To be close to remaining family, her sister and brother-in-law in particular, Sterling transferred to Emory University. When Blythe had Christopher, their lives were bright again. But the joy was short-lived when her nephew suffered a sudden illness and died. The damage to her family was irreparable.

Sterling returned to the living room and sat on the one section of couch not piled high with clothes and magazines. She heard a noise beneath her and, suddenly, a black cat slithered out. The frightened feline looked up at Sterling with amber eyes, meowing low and long.

"Raven, right? Oh, you poor thing?" Sterling reached down and stroked the cat. "Shhh, Raven, don't worry. I'll protect you. Hmm, what's this?"

The cat tried to dislodge a foreign object stuck in her left paw. Sterling picked up the cat and saw a piece of bloodied human skin.

"Raven, it looks like you met Harry's killer."

She cradled the cat and absorbed the living room. The furnishings were old, and the rugs on the hardwoods were thin and worn. Every item in the room had been disturbed – probably a struggle between Harry and the killer. Beneath the mantle, photos documenting Harry's life were strewn like pieces of a jigsaw puzzle of faraway locales. She spied the Grand Canyon, the Vegas strip, and even Big Ben in London, but Sterling saw no photos of children.

Raven curled up on her lap and went to sleep. A bit later, Sterling heard a clock chime, 8:00 am, from somewhere in the back of the house. She slid Raven onto a cushion and picked up the phone receiver on the end table beside them. Somehow it survived the apparent scuffle.

Sterling, you can do this. Stay calm. You have to protect your sister. It may be your only chance to save her and show her how much you love her.

She pressed the three numbers and heard a male voice say, "Baltimore 911, what's your emergency?"

"I need the police. I need to report a murder. A Mr. Harry Brown, of 869 Vine Street Baltimore. My name is Sterling Barrington. I just found Mr. Brown at his home. No, no, I'm fine. Please just send someone here." She hung up the phone and sighed.

"Raven, I'll bet your hungry. Let's see what I can find."

Sterling went into the kitchen, and the cat followed her. She didn't want to destroy the crime scene further, so she tore a paper towel off the dispenser and used it to open the cabinets. She pulled out a small bowl and looked for some cat food. Inside the pantry, she found a large bag of dry cat food. The sack had been ripped and the last of the food spilled on to the floor. She filled the bowl and offered it to Raven.

Twenty long minutes passed before Sterling heard cars pull up to the house. She looked out the front window and saw a plain brown

Chevrolet sedan and a black van that read Anne Arundel County

Crime Scene Unit on its side.

Remember, Sterling. You're doing this for Blythe.

The police knocked on the door and called out as they entered.

"Baltimore PD, coming in."

"In here Officers,"

"Ms. Barrington, is it?"

"Yes."

"I'm Detective Dan Keegan, this is Detective Maria Angelo

and these people are the crime scene unit. Guy's, I'll take Ms.

Barrington's statement over here, you start processing the body."

"Ms. Barrington, why don't you tell us what happened to, Mr.

Brown is it?"

"Yes, Harry Brown. I don't know what happened. I work in

DC at The Franklin Energy Institute and came to see Mr. Brown

about a business matter. I needed his input on a part of the Energy Bill

that's going to vote soon."

"Why didn't you meet with him at his office or your office?"

"Mr. Brown is... I mean he retired from the DOE. He didn't

have an office anymore."

"Why couldn't he come to your office?"

"His health wouldn't permit it."

"Is that your car out front?

"Yes, I drove here this morning."

"This morning? Have you been here before?"

"Yes, for a brief introductory meeting. This morning, I saw the front door open and called out. When no one answered, I worried something had happened to him. So, I entered the house and discovered his body."

"Ok, then. What have you touched in the house?"

"I think, just the door, the phone, the couch, the cat food and, oh, and the cat. That reminds me I want to show you something."

"Ok, but we'll have to take your fingerprints. What do you want to show me?"

Raven wandered back into the living room licking her lips. Sterling reached down, picked up the cat, and held out her paw toward the detective.

"I think this might be important, maybe from the killer?"

"Interesting. Hey Benjy, come see this. Take whatever it is out of the paw and see if we come up with anything. DNA, maybe? Be sure and run the feline DNA tests too. If this cat has the killers' DNA, then the killer has the cat's DNA. We didn't buy that high-tech machine for nothing. Also, get Ms. Barrington's fingerprints."

Detective Keegan turned to his partner and said "Maria, call the ME to get an ETA, then examine the property exterior. Ms. Barrington, did you go anywhere else in the house? With the house tossed like this, it looks like someone wanted something. Have any idea what that might be?"

"I found the house like this when I got here." Sterling wiped the ink from her hand with a tissue the crime scene investigator gave her.

"You didn't see anyone else when you got here, Ms. Barrington?"

"No, whoever did this left before I got here."

"Write your contact information on this pad for me. I may need to ask you more questions later. Does Mr. Brown have any living relatives, an emergency contact?"

"I don't know anything about his family situation. I knew he retired from the DOE and his wife died years ago. In fact, could I take the cat with me? I don't want it to be given to a shelter."

"Just a minute, hey Benjy, are you through with the cat?"

"Yeah, I'm done," the crime scene investigator said.

"Ok, I don't have a problem with that. I'll be in touch."

The investigator handed the cat to Sterling.

"Thank you, Detective."

"Miss Barrington, you don't have any travel plans in the near future, do you?"

"No, Detective. I'll be in the area. I hope you find out who did this to Harry and why. He did not deserve to go like this."

CHAPTER NINE

The cab pulled up to the front of the Georgetown Café. Walker paid the driver and walked inside. Clean, cheap, and off the beaten path. The eatery opened in the 1950's and looked like it had been pulled right out of the movie, American Graffiti.

Walker headed for a back booth, passing a few people at the counter, but saw no one of significance. A tired waitress took scratched down his order, black coffee. He lit a new cigarette and tapped it on the ashtray.

I can't let the truth become public now. I've got too much invested. Diabetes may be stronger than I am, but that Southern bitch will be stopped.

Walker grew up destitute in the coal-mining region of England. His mother died during the birth of her fourth child. His Father, a coal miner, devastated at the death of his wife, worked all day and frequented pubs at night.

Walker, or Wally as he went by then, was the eldest and at just twelve years old, took over the parenting of his siblings. He skipped school and scavenged food for them. After a few weeks, the neighbors turned his father into the authorities. Wally and his brothers were placed in separate foster homes. They never saw each other again.

Not book smart, but clever, Walker cheated his way to a full scholarship at the University of Birmingham and bribed his way to a Master of Electrical Engineering at Cambridge. After graduation, he worked for the Royal Academy of Sciences (RAS) in magnetic and radiation research.

At that year's Institute of Electrical and Electronic Engineers convention in Stockholm, the housing boom across the UK and the U.S. had the members concerned. More homes meant more electric generation. More generation meant more power plants, substations, and power lines to provide electricity to these homes.

The electric industry in both countries needed to know the impact power lines would have when installed in close proximity to homes, schools and workplaces. Were there any negative safety or health-related side effects?

Walker became a team member of a joint task force with the U.S. DOE. At the first joint meeting he met an American from the DOE, Harry Brown. The task force performed experiments on the effects EMFs generated by power lines had on living beings when near them.

First, they used field mice. Their results proved EMFs caused several types of cancer. Next, they needed to know if humans were affected the same way.

In England, Walker posed as a census taker to question people who lived and worked near transmission lines, towers and substations, to find out if they had any illnesses or deaths in their families.

His results in the UK documented numerous accounts of cancers, stillborn births, and sterility. Harry came to the same conclusion in the U.S. EMFs, if close to humans, caused illnesses and deaths.

The task force members were required to sign a confidentiality agreement that would prevent the catastrophic results from ever going public and told to turn in all notes. The results were sealed in a safe at the RAS.

The RAS and the DOE knew if the truth were revealed, there would be a worldwide revolt. Transmission lines would be toppled, substations destroyed, and power plants stormed. Then the lawsuits would begin. The industry would never recover financially from wrongful death and other lawsuits. And, no doubt, the public would demand and enforce new regulations, requiring the electric industry to erect power lines a safe distance away from citizens. The cost to relocate entire electricity networks would make companies fold. Both agencies agreed, the truth must be kept secret.

After this EMF study, Walker took his first vacation. He travelled to Greece, where he met his future wife; Eileen Berman, a rich American, and recent graduate of Smith College. She adored Walker, and he realized she would be his ticket to a better life. He courted her long distance, and eventually her family paid for his move to the States.

Unbeknownst to his superiors, Walker kept copies of his EMF study notes and horrific conclusions. He brought them with him to the States.

He and Ellen married, and her father used his contacts to get Walker a job at The Franklin. Eileen got fatter after the birth of each child and stopped making an effort to be attractive. Walker never loved her. He had numerous affairs and drank to fill his void. He lived the life he believed he deserved. No one would ruin that for him.

No one indeed, but diabetes and dementia were trying to topple his empire. He had no control over his mind and body anymore. The memory loss, deteriorating eyesight and muscle weakness grew worse every month. As a "Fuck you" to his illness, he continued to smoke and drink, against doctor's orders. He hadn't revealed his condition to any family or colleagues.

How long can I keep up this health charade?

Walker heard the Senator's Escalade before he saw it. The Cadillac's tires spewed gravel on the window outside of Walker's booth. The Senator's aide, Vinnie Tirello, built like a tree trunk, stepped out of the driver's door and opened the Senator's door.

The Senator marched into the diner wearing an expensive black leather coat. Vinnie followed the Senator, scanning the premises for troublemakers. He remained standing toward the back of the restaurant, keeping an eye on everything, sidearm strapped to his belt.

"Put that god dam cigarette out, Walker. I don't want smoke in my face. Now, what's the problem?" The Senator slid his coat over the back of the booth.

Walker took one last drag and crushed the cigarette in the ashtray.

"Do you remember my VP of PR, Sterling Barrington? Well, the bitch found out something that could ruin our plans for the Energy Bill."

The Senator's eyes widened as he listened to Walker reveal what transpired. He took a drink from the small water glass on the table and swallowed hard.

"Shit. So, the Brown guy's been handled. Good. We will not let anyone stop the passage of this bill. We've worked too hard to get it to vote. I must have more power lines for my state. I won't stand for another blackout. My constituents went through hell. Call me as soon as you go through Ms. Barrington's office and find those documents. Then we'll decide how to handle her. By the way, did you know she's screwing one of my committee members, Congressman Reese from Georgia?"

"No, I didn't. What should we do about that?"

"I'll take care of Reese." The Senator wiped his hands with a paper napkin, crumpled it, and tossed it on the table. "Keep me apprised of any new details. Come on, Vinnie, I'm ready to go. Walker, wait awhile before you leave."

Walker nodded and took out a new cigarette. The Senator and Vinnie pulled out of the parking lot into the rainy, foggy DC night. Lightning brightened the sky. He lit his cigarette, took a drag, and waved to the waitress to bring another cup of coffee. He smiled; confident he saved the Energy Bill, and his career.

CHAPTER TEN

Blythe walked out of Harry's house, leaving Sterling to deal with the police.

I couldn't risk being arrested. Sterling will keep me out of this mess. Right?

She walked two blocks, tightly clutching her bag while surveying the area for people. The darkness and uneven sidewalk did not make it easy.

Would it ever cool off? Atlanta's weather isn't this bad.

She reached her beat-up car, which she'd left unlocked. Back in Atlanta, she'd driven a new Mercedes every year. When her son, Christopher, died, material possessions and status symbols stopped mattering.

If somebody wants this used pile of junk, they can help themselves. There's always another way to get where I'm going.

Blythe got in the car, turned off her cell phone and started driving. She didn't want to talk to Carter yet or discuss tonight's event.

She passed a giant substation, the EMFs from which probably killed Harry's wife, and left Baltimore for Virginia, keeping to the speed limit. Power lines stalked her the whole way.

They're everywhere.

She checked the rearview mirror for law enforcement vehicles and headed for the SAFEPOWER team house, decided against it, and passed the exit. She needed time to reflect on the last few hours.

How would Carter take the news about Harry's death? I can't tell him about Sterling. Would the police believe Sterling? Will my secret come out?

She exited the highway onto a feeder road, parked, opened the door and vomited. She wiped her mouth, turned the air conditioner to high and leaned her head against the headrest.

Blythe admired and resented Sterling for being able to stay clearheaded in stressful situations. When their parents were killed, Sterling returned home from college and took charge of the situation. She made funeral arrangements and handled estate matters. When Christopher became ill with leukemia, Sterling took care of Blythe's domestic duties to ensure she focused on her sweet, dear boy.

Before Christopher's death, Blythe believed Sterling loved her unconditionally. Then, her sister left when she needed her most. She left to work for the enemy, the industry that killed her beloved son.

Could she trust her again?

Blythe drove to a nearby gas station, filled the car with half a tank and went inside to pay. She bought a cup of what appeared to be coffee and tossed cash at the attendant. The strong bitter brew cleared her head.

Located a half mile south of the Potomac River in Fairfax County, Virginia, Fort Marcy Park protected DC during the Civil War. Now a part of the National Park Service, it was a true oasis with trees that reached to the sky, budding plants and hiking trails. Soothing sounds of the Potomac River murmured in the distance.

She came here to be alone, meditate, and reminisce about Christopher.

Today, the parking lot held three cars and an Arlington County school bus. She found an empty park bench and wiped the rainwater from the seat. Droplets on the leaves sparkled all around her.

This paradise also had a dark side. In July 1993, the body of Deputy White House Counsel Vince Foster (of the Clinton

Administration) was discovered in his car. Officials ruled his death a suicide by self-inflicted gunshot. However, three federal judges added witness intimidation and murder evidence to the official report. After this morning's events, Blythe thought of Vince Foster.

Did Vince have deep dark secrets that he wanted to publicize, like Harry? Did someone silence him? Harry wanted to tell the truth, and someone killed him to keep it hidden.

She pulled out a worn paper fan from her bag and smiled. She and Christopher were in an Atlanta dime store when he saw the fan. He loved the garish shapes and panda bears painted on it and had used his allowance money to buy it.

"For the best Mommy in the world," he said presenting it proudly to her.

Tears welled in her eyes. She kept it with her all the time and taped the folds to keep it whole. She fanned herself and caressed the locket around her neck that housed Christopher's photograph.

My precious boy. I wanted justice for you, but more lives have been lost, not saved.

She sipped the last of her coffee and set the cup on the bench, absorbing the sounds of birds, cicadas, and children's voices nearby. A drop of rain fell from a leaf above and landed on her cheek.

About twenty children, around eight years old, walked across the park toward her. They appeared to be part of a class field trip identifying trees, plants, bugs. Christopher would have been their age by now. A few boys tried to run ahead.

"Tommy, Jason, come back here right now. No running. Get back in line. Children, hold hands with your partner. Now, who can tell me what this is?" the young female teacher said to the class as she held up an acorn.

Would the sadness ever lessen?

After years of infertility tests and miscarriages, Blythe had finally welcomed a perfect little blonde angel into her world. No one understood her pain when he was taken away. Not her husband. Not Sterling. In her darkest hour, she only received support from her SAFEPOWER family. They too believed that EMFs murdered her angel.

She agreed with their cause. Murders resulting from EMF exposure must end. No more power lines could be built. At first, she refused to participate in protests. She worried about their methods, namely their use of violence. Carter told her the violent attacks would get the electric companies' attention.

Carter had the next attack planned for tonight. This time they would hit multiple substations in Virginia and Maryland. Carter impressed upon her the importance of participating. They were an army with a peaceful agenda, but to achieve peace, the enemy must be stopped. Collateral damage, or innocent lives lost, would be an unfortunate side effect to achieve their goal. She wondered if she could even participate in the planned violence. After all they did for her, she didn't want to leave the SAFEPOWER family. Where else could she go and who else could possibly understand?

Sterling called us radicals. I don't want anyone to get hurt, but maybe this is the only way to get them to stop.

Blythe opened her bag and pulled out a worn overstuffed manila envelope, holding it like a rare jewel.

Harry's evidence. The proof that EMFs cause cancer. I couldn't tell Sterling I found them. With Carter's new frame of mind, I'm not ready to turn it over to him, either.

She drove out of the Park and looked for somewhere to hide Harry's notes. Then she saw it, the Vienna Metro Station. She went into the lobby and found lockers for rent, placing Harry's documents inside an empty one. With locker key secured safely in her locket, Blythe left the station and headed back to her real family.

CHAPTER ELEVEN

Sterling left Harry's house with Raven in her arms. The damp morning air made her flushed face tingle. The police questions were tough.

She mechanically opened the car door, placed Raven on the passenger seat and took off for DC, mind racing.

If Blythe didn't kill Harry, who did? Who else knew he had the damning research about EMFs? It must be someone in the industry. Someone I know.

A car honked and swerved around her.

Damn, pay attention Sterling.

She pulled over and turned on her cell phone. Six new voicemail messages, 5 from Toni asking her to call the office and one from Trevor. She called Trevor first.

"Congressman Reese's office."

"Beth, this is Sterling. Is he in?"

"No, he's in a committee meeting and won't be available until later this afternoon," the young intern said.

"Ok, tell him I called."

She needed to speak with Blythe again.

She dialed The Franklin. "Toni, it's Sterling. I took care of some personal business this morning. I'll be in before lunch. Anything I need to know?"

"We wondered where you were. Your presentation's this afternoon. Walker's nervous as a cat about the board meeting. Let's see. Not much else going on here. Oh, yeah, SAFEPOWER sent out a press release."

"What does it say?"

"It's a reminder about their candlelight vigil on the Mall tomorrow."

"That's all?"

"Were you expecting something else?"

"No, I thought it would be something new. Tell Walker, I'm ready for this afternoon. See you in a while."

At least SAFEPOWER is doing something non-violent for a change. Blythe, please stay out of trouble.

She went to her apartment and got Raven settled. She placed a blanket on the laundry room floor with some tuna and water in bowls.

"I hope you like it here Raven. I know you miss Harry."

She took a quick shower then dressed in her navy pinstripe power suit and pumps. The board would notice her even if they didn't pay attention to her presentation. She gave Raven one last pat on the way out.

Back in her office, Sterling reviewed her meeting notes.

Focus, Sterling, focus. I have to defend the industry until I find Harry's documents. No one can know what happened over the last 24 hours.

She heard a cough and looked up.

"What're you doing?" Sandy said leaning against her door frame.

"Sandy, I'm busy. Do you have a question for me?"

"No. What is that?"

"I'm preparing for my presentation to the board. What do you want? By the way, you look terrible."

"Thanks for noticing. I didn't get much sleep last night. I, uh, had a date with this hot Asian chick. We fucked all over my condo. So, Sterling, when will you be ready for some of my action?"

"I'm not interested in you or your sex life. Leave me alone. I have work to finish."

"So, I'm not good enough for you. I'll bet that Congressman is getting some, isn't he?"

"My personal life is none of your business. Now, get the hell out of here and close the door behind you."

Sandy glared at her, turned around and slammed her office door, causing the frame to shake.

Just what I need right now, that slime hitting on me again.

It wouldn't do any good for her to complain about Sandy's behavior to anyone at The Franklin. Even in the 21st century, this industry retained its good-old boy attitude. Women were not treated as equals. She shook off his verbal attack and continued reviewing her notes.

Moments later, Sterling walked up the open interior staircase of The Franklin to the board room. She stood at the back while Walker finished his marketing update. Seated around the mahogany conference table were twelve of the country's most powerful men, CEOs of the largest, formerly regulated, electric utilities in the country. There were no female CEOs.

Paintings of former board members hung on the conference room walls, with Ben Franklin's portrait at the back of the room. He seemed to be watching the proceedings, ready to say, "What have you done to my electricity?"

These men, eager for the new Energy Bill to be passed, were here to discuss the status of said bill and radical environmental groups. They were weary of customer complaints about high bills, bad service, and now, safety.

Walker's words were slurred and thick, his comments vague and unclear about The Franklin marketing program.

What's wrong with him? Is he drunk? Is that why he's been acting so strange lately?

"Without further ado, here she is gentlemen, our campaign director, Sterling," Walker said as he gestured to her. Sterling felt herself being eyed up and down by the men as she walked to the front of the room.

"Well, at least you got someone good looking to do the job, but does she have the balls to take on these wackos?" said Beau LaFontaine, CEO of New Orleans Electric.

"Before you pass judgment on me, listen to my presentation and then ask your questions," Sterling said.

"Whew, she's a spitfire! I like that. Ok, little lady. We'll listen to you. Settle down boys, let's hear her out," said John Bradley of Wyoming Electric.

"Walker, please turn off the lights." The PowerPoint presentation illuminated her lovely silhouette in the dark room.

"Gentlemen, meet the enemy, SAFEPOWER. We've dealt with environmental groups before, but never one so bold or, we suspect, so violent. The Feds believe, and we at The Franklin concur, that they blew up the Ohio substation last month. Smart and maniacal, they left behind no evidence. They believe, and want the American public to believe, that EMFs from power lines cause cancer. My job is to protect your interests. In your packets you will find copies of press releases I'll be sending out to combat their negative statements as well as bill stuffers for your customers to read about electricity benefits and safety. This campaign will be positive. We will not sink to their level. Also, SAFEPOWER will be holding a candlelight vigil on the Mall tomorrow evening, in their words, to honor those who died of cancer due to our industry. The Franklin president, Robert Pittman, will hold a press conference the same day, announcing the donation of $1 million to the American Cancer Society, as a token of goodwill."

Comments of "Sounds good, it's about time, and let's get this to the customers ASAP," were heard from the men. Sterling left the Board Room satisfied she'd convinced the CEOs and Walker.

Walker had watched her intensely during the presentation and nodded at her as she left the board room.

Why is he looking at me like that? Did Walker know Harry?

Did Walker kill Harry?

CHAPTER TWELVE

Famous for its crime, District Heights in Prince Georges County held the title for 75% of murders in Maryland. Carter Thompson waited in The Elbow Room for his mentor and financial backer, the Speaker of the House, Matthew Sinclair, to arrive. He sat in the last booth of the L-shaped dive bar; small, dark, and dirty. A faded dart board hung on the wall to his right and a worn pool table sat on his left.

Carter folded the Washington Post and laid it on the table then took a clean handkerchief from his pocket and wiped the rim of his beer bottle. He grimaced at the thought of how many germs were in this place. Sinclair had picked this spot because, as the Speaker, he wanted to ensure no one saw them together. So, every time they met, it was in a different, out-of-the-way, grungy haunt for lowlifes.

Carter took in the bar's occupants. There were a few drunks, heads in their whiskeys, not likely to recognize their own reflections and certainly not the Speaker.

He met Sinclair, a liberal from Vermont, ten years ago when he ran for a representative's seat in the Vermont House but lost. At the time, Congressman Sinclair liked what he saw in Carter and hired

him. Carter became his chief of special projects, which included

taking incriminating photos of an opponent, or anyone else who

caused him trouble, or planting evidence about Sinclair's enemies.

Carter also watched over Sinclair's mistress du jour. He

escorted the young women to public events so Sinclair could have his

mistress at the same events he and his wife attended. Carter's life

revolved around Sinclair's bidding and he wouldn't have it any other

way.

Heir to the oldest and largest Vermont maple syrup business,

Sinclair's grandfather invented the dripless spout for their bottles.

With no money worries, he went into politics to save his statesmen,

and now his countrymen from the arch conservatives and big business

that he believed corrupted America.

He whitewashed to the press, the severe impact on his state

when he sold the family company to a Japanese conglomerate.

Several plants were shut down and thousands of jobs were lost.

Sinclair distributed petty severances to long-term employees and, to

keep the unions happy, he donated $1 million dollars to their

retirement fund. Just a drop in the maple bucket for him, but it kept his voters happy. In his heart, Sinclair believed he did the right thing. The added fortune enabled him to give more to his foundation, and as a result, help more people.

Currently, Sinclair was the most vocal House member against the Energy Bill. He believed the power industry refused to admit that EMFs kill people and touted alternative methods of electricity production. To prove this, he invested in a Vermont wind generation farm.

When the electric industry deregulated in the 1990's, Sinclair secretly created SAFEPOWER with Carter acting as the public organization head. Only the two of them knew Sinclair funded the project. There was no paper trail linking him to the group.

Sinclair sweated the threat of more power lines being built if the Energy Bill passed. He used his influence in the House to gain votes against it but didn't know if he had the votes needed to stop the bill's passage.

Sinclair instructed Carter to take stronger measures that made power providers take notice, thus the attacks on substations began.

A beam of light poured into the dark room. Carter looked up and saw the Speaker walk into the bar, head tucked down and shoulders hunched. He was wearing a faded baseball cap, stained khakis and a worn blue Izod shirt. Nothing could really disguise his lean, regal frame. Carter nodded as the Speaker slid into the booth and pushed a Sam Adams bottle toward him.

"So, where do we stand with this Brown guy?" Sinclair said. He took a swig of the beer.

"Blythe met with him late last night. She'll be at the team's house this evening before our next project. I'll get the documents from her then."

"Did it go down all right?"

"I haven't called her. That way, no phone records."

"Yes, good idea. As soon as you get them, call me. Is everything in place for tonight?"

"Everything's in the vans, and we're ready to go. I plan to have Blythe go with us."

"You like her, don't you?"

"What? No, no, only as a fellow supporter. She shares our belief that power companies are killers."

"We've come this far, don't let emotions cloud your focus. We've got a job to do."

"Yes sir, I know."

"Good, if there's a problem tonight, get rid of everything and leave the house."

"I know the drill. It'll be fine, just like the others."

"We're going to stop this Energy Bill," the Speaker took another swallow of beer and got out of the booth. "I'll look for fireworks in the Southern skies tonight."

CHAPTER THIRTEEN

Sandy slammed his fists on his desk, scattering papers and upending an old cup of coffee.

That bitch, Sterling. She rejected me, AGAIN. And she didn't even mention Harry.

He hurled his stapler across the office, where it dented the opposite wall with a loud thud.

I've got to talk to Walker, but he's in that damn board meeting.

He pulled his Blackberry out of its holster and texted Walker.

"Need to do something. Can't sit still."

"Stay calm. Keep your mouth shut. I've got everything under control. I'll call you later," Walker replied.

Screw this! I'm out of here.

Sandy walked to the lobby and pushed the elevator button, tightly gripping his briefcase. Someone tapped his shoulder as the elevator dinged. He turned around to see the cherubic face and bald head of Bob Turner.

Sandy put his hand against the elevator door to keep it open and surveyed Bob, becoming aroused. Bob's tailored suit accentuated his buff physique.

"Bad day? Let me buy you a drink," Bob said.

"Yeah, that'd be good."

They went next door to 701 Restaurant, a frequent hangout of The Franklin staff, FBI, and other government workers. Sandy didn't worry about being seen with Bob there. They were just two co-workers at happy hour.

Some engineers from The Franklin sitting at a table said hello as they entered. Sandy nodded to them and continued to the bar with Bob. They squeezed up to the counter to order drinks and leaned into each other while conversing. Sandy could feel the electricity between them. The combination of scotch, light conversation, and lust helped him forget about Sterling. Bob grazed Sandy's hand when he reached for the bowl of pretzels.

"Want to go somewhere quiet to continue our conversation?" Bob said.

"Yeah, that sounds like a good idea."

"I know just the place."

Sandy swigged the rest of his scotch and paid the bill. He waved off Bob's attempt to pull out his wallet.

"I've got it. Where to?"

"I live a couple of blocks down on 6th. That ok?"

"Fine with me."

Sandy awoke to the sound of running water. Groggy, he looked around the room and rubbed his head.

Where am I?

He felt the space next to him, still warm. The clock on the nightstand read 6:00 am.

Oh, shit. What did I do?

He untwisted himself from the sheets and got out of bed. He found his underwear, shirt and pants.

Where the hell were his socks?

Sandy got down on all fours and looked under the bed. In the corner, wound around a bedpost, he saw one sock. He shook the bedcovers and found the other sock between the duvet and top sheet.

No more scotch on an empty stomach.

He dressed, ran his hands through his hair, and walked into the bathroom. In the jacuzzi tub, amidst a mound of bubbles, lounged Bob. The radio played seventies music.

"Good morning, sexy. Come on in, the water's perfect," Bob said. He smiled and blew some bubbles off his hand toward Sandy. "Did you have fun last night? I know I did."

"I drank too much. This won't happen again. I'm leaving now."

"So, you're a closet queen. Your secret's safe with me, lover. We can have fun together." Bob reached his wet hand out toward Sandy.

"You fucking fag. Yeah, you'll keep my secret."

Sandy's hand tightened into a fist. Bob's eyes filled with fear. He tried to climb out of the jacuzzi, but slipped back into the water, and hit his head on the back of the tub.

"Ow, God damn it. Just get the hell out of here and leave me alone. Coward."

"Nobody calls me a coward."

Sandy's eyes scoured the bathroom for a weapon. On the counter, next to the tub, he spied a stereo plugged into the wall. He grabbed it and threw it into the jacuzzi.

"No!"

Bob's body convulsed with the impact of the electrical current and sucked him under the water. Sparks and smoke rose from the tub. It only took a few moments for him to die. The room smelled like seared flesh and burnt hair.

Now, my secret is safe.

Sandy grabbed a bath towel off the wall rack and walked around the condo, wiping off items he could've touched. He took the sheets off the bed and placed them by the front door.

He returned to the bathroom and looked at the tub. Bob's body swelled in the water, with the stereo unit wedged behind him.

Shit.

He reached into the tub for the radio and lost his balance.

Fuck, fuck, fuck.

His pants were soaked from the knees down. Bob's body wouldn't budge.

Sandy found a mop in the kitchen and used it like a plunger to force Bob's body away from the unit. He retrieved the stereo, which had come unplugged during the violent electrocution, dried it, and placed it back in its original spot on the counter, then returned the mop to pantry.

What else?

He walked over to the front door and looked through the peephole, seeing an empty hallway. He stuffed the towel and sheets in his briefcase and left.

It's easier the second time.

CHAPTER FOURTEEN

Blythe left the Vienna Metro Station and drove to the SAFEPOWER house. Her head ached. She'd been thinking too much about the upcoming protest, whether to participate or not. She'd also been mulling over what to tell Carter about Harry's death and his notes.

She turned down a dark, snake-like farm road in a wooded, secluded part of Loudon County, Virginia. Its rolling hills, rushing streams and tall trees housed many large expensive horse farms.

Her headlights followed the curves of the rural road. Something jumped in front of her car. She braked and caught her breath, hoping she'd stopped in time. In the middle of the lane were a doe and her baby. They stood still and looked at her with bright eyes then ran into the brush.

Mama deer, protect your baby.

She found the SAFEPOWER driveway, turned in and stopped the car. She leaned out the window to punch in the code of the day and nodded to the surveillance camera on the post above the gate. Carter was obsessed with security.

She pulled through the entrance and the gate closed behind her. At the end of the unlit driveway, unseen from the farm road, stood the SAFEPOWER headquarters. Home sweet home.

The building appeared dark and empty due to the blackout curtains inside, but Blythe knew there was an army in there preparing for battle.

Carter had converted an old red barn into their headquarters and barracks. Functional and utilitarian, it served their purpose with no flourishes or fancy amenities. He divided the building into a few rooms: a living area, kitchen, two large bedrooms with bunk beds and dorm-like baths. One room for men, the other for women. Couples were separated. Carter's office was in the upstairs loft.

Carter insisted his supporters focus on their objective and not be distracted by outside influences. They were allowed to watch television, but only the news channels. Their mission, to stop the passage of the Energy Bill and force power providers to confess that EMFs kill.

Blythe walked by several black panel vans on her way to the front door. She stood in the entry hall listening to Carter give a pep talk in the great room. Its peaked, beamed ceiling made Carter's voice sound like a powerful preacher in a sanctuary. He stood on the hearth with his team gathered around, mesmerized. His blonde hair and blue eyes made him look like a poster boy for the Aryan nation.

Carter nodded to her and continued his speech. He was a masterful speaker who truly believed in their cause. She smiled at him. She had joined SAFEPOWER after hearing him speak at a protest and fully believed he would get justice for Christopher's unnecessary death.

"Tonight, we launch the second phase of our Awareness Plan: to strike multiple substations in Virginia and Maryland. Thanks to our first successful action in Ohio, we're prepared and ready. We've gone over every step, timed our actions down to the second, nothing left to chance. After tonight, the power companies and the left-wing radicals will know we will not stand by silently while more power lines are built, and more innocent victims murdered. For some of you, tonight will be your first time participating. We welcome you. You've trained, you've rehearsed and you're ready. Everyone knows the plan. I will give the signal by phone. If there's a problem at your site, abort. Any questions? Good. Good. SAFEPOWER will make its mark on history and our intentions will be known around the world. Killers will be punished for their crimes!"

The team members clapped. A chant of "SAFEPOWER, SAFEPOWER" resounded in the room. Carter beamed at his loyal followers.

He worked his way through the team members, shook hands, patted shoulders, then moved over to Blythe. Carter smiled at her and took her hand in his.

"There you are. We were worried about you. How did the meeting go with Mr. Brown? Let's go to my office. I've got to see his notes." He led her to his office and shut the door.

"Hand them over. I can't wait any longer. Tell me everything."

"I don't have his notes."

"Why not? What happened?"

"I found Harry dead when I got there. I left as fast as I could and have been driving around for the last few hours."

Carter dropped her hand, rolled his eyes and sat down in the closest chair. "Holy crap. Brown's dead? Our ace in the hole? His industry found out. They killed him. Okay, this is just a minor setback. We'll continue with our timetable. We'll get justice in other ways."

"I, I don't know if I can do this tonight, Carter. After what happened to Harry, I don't think I'm up to it."

"You're coming tonight. Now more than ever, we can't let those bastards win. We have to show them we aren't afraid. No matter how many substations we have to blow up."

"But innocent people will be without power. Should we really do that to them?"

"Blythe, we aren't the bad guys. We're not killers. The electric industry is the problem. Nothing bad will happen. You'll see."

"Maybe you're right. Okay, I'll go with the team."

"That's the spirit." Carter patted her on the back. They left his office and walked back to the great room.

Carter clapped his hands. "Ok, let's move out."

The ten teams went to their respective black panel vans. Blythe and her team members, four men and two women, climbed into the back of theirs. They sat on the floor cross-legged. One of the women handed her black greasepaint to smear on her face as the others had done. With their dark clothes and blackened faces, only the whites of their eyes were seen in the darkness. No one spoke as they headed to their target.

Their substation target, located in Culpepper County, Virginia, sat next to an industrial park. They stopped across the street from the facility while Carter checked the area from the passenger window with his night vision binoculars.

"Ok, we're clear. Let's go."

Outside the van, he motioned to the group to gather around him. He took a revolver out of his pocket, tightened the silencer, and shot out the lone streetlight. The glass from the streetlight shattered and rained to the ground.

They each pulled night vision goggles from their jackets and positioned them on their faces. The team's second in command, Mike Moore, handed out AK-47s. Carter waved his hand forward and they walked toward their appointed target.

I'm doing the right thing. I'm doing the right thing.

She gripped her weapon, afraid any sudden movement might make it fire.

This is for Christopher. You can do this.

Carter cut the chain and bolt that held the gate closed. Past attacks had showed them that power substations never used security guards, guard dogs or sophisticated alarm systems.

If we could do this, what's stopping foreign terrorists from attacking the grid?

The team followed Carter into the compound to the center of the facility and stood guard as their leader wired the bomb to the substation's main control panel.

It took two minutes to connect, but it seemed like hours to Blythe. Carter nodded to the team when he finished. In single file, they left the substation. Waiting a moment at the entrance, Mike, scoured the area for any unwelcome visitors, and waved the team out.

They got back into the van and drove off, stopping a few blocks away.

Carter called the other team leaders for a status report. All the teams had completed their tasks and awaited the go-ahead command from Carter.

"Okay, in 60 seconds detonate. Start the countdown now," Carter said to the teams on the phone.

"You do the honors, Blythe," Carter said. He handed her the remote-control device for the bomb.

"Just push this button and your justice will be served," Mike said.

Her hands trembled when handed the remote. "Now?"

"Now," Carter said.

"For you, Christopher. Your life will not be forgotten."

She heard the blast and saw fire and sparks shoot out of the substation into the dark sky. She smiled for the first time since Christopher's death.

CHAPTER FIFTEEN

"Breaking news. Virginia Electric and Maryland Power announced a massive power outage across both states due to violent attacks on ten substations. Thousands of customers have been affected. There was one fatality reported in Culpepper County, Virginia. A Virginia Electric security guard was killed by an explosion. The man's name is being withheld pending notification of his family. The Virginia Electric attacks, and subsequent murder, were recorded on new security cameras. We will now air the video Virginia Electric shared with us. You can see a team of six breaking into the substation. It is not clear whether these individuals were male or female due to their black clothing and face paint. This is the first substation attack for Maryland Power and the third attack for Virginia Electric. Both power providers stated they will work around the clock to return power to customers. Crews from Penn Electric and West Virginia Power arrived this morning to help with the outage. FBI investigators released a statement saying the radical environmental group, SAFEPOWER, is considered the primary suspect in both attacks."

Sterling dropped her compact when she heard the announcement. She turned to watch the video.

Is that Blythe? Did she participate? Why did I let her leave Harry's?

She retrieved the fallen compact and sat on her bed. Raven purred and looked up at her. She rubbed her cramping stomach.

After what happened to Harry, why would Blythe participate in a violent act?

She stroked the cat curled up on a pillow beside her with one hand and reached for her cell with the other. She punched in Blythe's number. She got voicemail, again, and left another message.

"Blythe, please call me. Tell me you weren't a part of the um, activities last night."

She finished dressing, gave Raven her breakfast, then a final pat before leaving. Sterling was reaching for the door knob when her cell phone rang.

She dropped everything and pulled out her phone. Trevor, again. She let it ring.

How would she tell him about Blythe? Had it only been two days ago they went to that wonderful dinner?

Once at The Franklin, Sterling stayed in her office, away from Sandy and Walker, keeping busy with press releases and media scripts about the Energy Bill and the substation attacks.

She jumped when her intercom buzzed. Toni said, "Sterling, some of Baltimore's finest are here to see you. Shall I send them back?"

The police?

"Yes, Toni, send them back."

Sterling stood at her door and waited for the police to arrive. Detectives Keegan and Angelo walked into Sterling's office.

"Hello, detectives. Please have a seat."

"Hello, Ms. Barrington." Detective Keegan said.

Detective Keegan laid his raincoat over the back of a chair and sat while Detective Angelo looked around the office. Sterling shut the door and sat behind her desk.

They may have the surprise advantage, but it's my office, I'm in charge here.

"I hope you are here with good news. Do you have DNA results for the skin stuck in Raven's paw?"

"No, not yet. It's still in the lab. Baltimore is one of the few feline DNA labs in the country. If that cat scratched the killer, we'll find out. But, that's not why we're here."

"What can I do for you, detectives?"

"Obviously, we found your prints at the crime scene. However, we also found your business card. Why did Mr. Brown have it?"

"My card? Probably because I had a meeting with him before he died."

"I did some research on that new Energy Bill, the Bill that you said required Mr. Brown's input. If that Bill isn't passed, it could hurt the electric industry. Your industry. What did you meet with Mr. Brown about?"

"Not one thing, but several. You need to understand that his experience in the industry is invaluable, not only to me, but also to the upcoming Energy Bill vote."

"Let's move on. Detective Angelo, please tell Ms. Barrington what else we discovered at Mr. Brown's home."

"We found a bloody kitchen knife under the refrigerator covered in fingerprints. The knife edge matched the defensive wounds on Harry's hands. Our lab should be getting us the fingerprint and blood results today. Is there anything you'd like to tell us about this knife, Ms. Barrington?" Detective Angelo looked up from her notepad.

"I don't know anything about a knife. I certainly didn't see one when I found Harry's body."

"Are you sure? It's better for you to tell us now. The Assistant District Attorney is even willing to make a deal if you cooperate sooner rather than later. Maybe we should continue this at our office?" Detective Keegan said.

"Continue what? Am I under arrest?"

"No, not at the moment."

"Then, I have nothing more to say without an attorney. Please leave."

"Ok, for now. But you must have wanted something badly enough from Harry to kill him. We'll find out what that was and be in touch, Ms. Barrington."

"Good day, officers."

The detectives left her office. She shut the door behind them and slowly exhaled.

I've got to talk to Blythe. The police are going to find something soon and our stories need to be straight.

She called Blythe's cell phone and got voicemail.

"Blythe, it's me. The Baltimore police were just in my office. We have to talk. Meet me at Dolley's, 7:00 pm tonight. No excuses. Be there if you want my help."

CHAPTER SIXTEEN

Walker stepped out of his office and laid some papers on Toni's desk. Phones rang, the fax machine beeped, and employees walked the halls. Walker noticed two unfamiliar silhouettes leaving Sterling's office.

"Toni, who are those people and why don't I recognize them?" He walked behind her and began to rub her shoulders.

"Ooh, that feels good. Don't stop. Those were two Baltimore detectives who showed up out of the blue. Sterling must be in some kind of trouble for them to make an unscheduled office visit," Toni said.

"Shit. Police to see Miss Goody Two Shoes? What's going on? If you hear anything let me know." He gave her shoulders one last squeeze then walked to Sandy's office.

He shut the door behind him and Sandy jumped.

"What the fuck's wrong with you? You're too jumpy. You're acting guilty. Did those Baltimore police question you too?"

"What Baltimore police?"

"Just now, two of them questioned Sterling in her office. We've got to find out what they know and what she told them."

"No, they didn't question me. But, I'll find out."

"The man's coming in today for an update. I'll buzz you when he gets here. You look terrible. Get some rest tonight, no fucking partying."

"Ok, ok. I'm fine."

Sandy swiveled his chair around to face the window. He looked at the Navy Memorial below. His eyes glazed over as he watched the fountains, water cascades soothing his frayed nerves.

Fucking hell. The police were here. How did they know about Sterling? If they found out about her, then they might find out about me being at Harry's. No, I wore gloves when I killed him and searched his house. I couldn't have left prints. They can't pin this on me. They won't find out about Bob either. I cleaned up after myself. No one will ever know I was at either place. Yeah, yeah, I'm fine.

****

Toni escorted Senator Morelli and Vincent to Walker's office. The Senator strutted down the hall. He waved and greeted The

Franklin employees along the way. He never let an opportunity to woo potential voters escape him. His presidential aspirations were no secret. He planned to announce his candidacy after the Energy Bill passed.

He walked by Sterling's office and noticed the closed door.

"Looks like Ms. Barrington's keeping her nose to the grindstone," the Senator said aloud as he neared Walker's office.

"Walker, hello, my good man. How are you?" The Senator extended his large hairy hand to Walker. He turned back to Vincent and said, "You wait out here. See that no one disturbs us," Vinnie nodded. He stood outside the office with his hands folded across his chest, eyes scanning the halls.

"Senator, please have a seat. Toni, go get Sandy and tell him the Senator is here. Close the door behind you."

"Sure thing, Walker. Nice to see you Senator," Toni said. She smiled with a coquettish grin then backed out the doorway. The Senator sat down at Walker's conference table.

"She's hot, Walker. Now that you're done with her, I may give her a go. So, where do we stand after our last meeting?"

"She's in a relationship now. Anyway, you really want to talk about this here?"

"Yes, your office isn't bugged. Unless you have something to tell me?"

"No, this office is clean."

"Ok, then. No one will know this is any different from the meetings I have here all the time."

"Yeah, I see what you mean. You're right."

"Of course, I'm right. That's why I'm the Senator and you're the lackey. So, update me on the Brown situation."

Walker's fists tightened around his coffee mug.

"No news on the location of Brown's notes. But, the Baltimore PD sent two plainclothes dicks here to question Sterling."

"Shit. Baltimore PD, hmm. Wait, this could help us. If the Baltimore PD thinks Sterling killed Harry, that's good for us. I have contacts in that precinct. I'll make some calls, find out what they know, and get back to you."

Two taps were heard on the office door and Sandy entered.

"Hello, Senator, good to see you. Don't get up."

"Sandy. Heard you did good work the other night. Don't think I'll forget it, either. I know loyalty when I see it."

The Senator stood up, shook hands with Sandy, and patted him on the back. Sandy smiled and sat down.

"Ok, moving on. I'll take care of the Baltimore PD. Where the fuck are Brown's notes? You've got to find them. There can't be any loose ends before this bill goes to vote. Capeesh?" The Senator leaned into the two men.

"We've got it under control, Tony. Besides, no one can tie you to Brown's death. Let me handle it," Walker said.

"It better be handled or we're all up shit creek. This is what I want you to do. Search her office. If you can't find Brown's documents, then go to her apartment. Take Vinnie if you need help. Do this tomorrow night. I'll handle Reese. As soon as you find the evidence, call me."

"Got it," Walker said.

"I'm not letting anyone stop the passage of the Energy Bill or ruin my plan to run for office. Is that understood? No one."

CHAPTER SEVENTEEN

A hidden jewel among the many treasured Washington museums, the National Portrait Gallery displayed portraits of historical figures, celebrities and other luminaries.

"Step over here, Miss," the security guard said to Sterling as she walked through the metal detector.

"Of course, sir."

She removed her Chanel chain link belt and handed it to the guard. He waved his wand over Sterling again.

"Ok, Miss, you can go ahead. Enjoy the gallery."

Would Blythe remember their special place?

Sterling had left Blythe a cryptic message in case SAFEPOWER listened to her voicemail. They needed to discuss recent events. It would only be a matter of days or even hours before the police discovered Sterling covered for Blythe at Harry's house. Either of them could be arrested for murder.

She hadn't been to the gallery since her move to DC, but she knew it well. Tears welled in her eyes as she strolled through the rooms absorbing the art. She stopped in front of a beautiful painting of Dolley Madison. Across the gallery, a well-dressed mother with two little girls, aged about six and eight, viewed a portrait of Paul Revere. They wore identical Lily Pulitzer dresses with matching hair bows.

The mother whispered something to the girls and they giggled, then walked hand in hand to the next room. Sterling smiled. She and Blythe were inseparable when they were young.

Would they ever be that close again?

During Sterling's youth, her family traveled to DC numerous times for her father's work. Her mother kept the girls busy by taking them to The Smithsonian, The National Gallery and The National Portrait Gallery. Along with the Hope Diamond, the two sisters' favorite DC attraction was the portrait of Dolley Madison at the National Portrait Gallery. The sisters enjoyed history and learning about the paintings' subjects. They relied on each other and shared everything.

Their world fell apart with the death of their parents and later Christopher's. Now they were estranged and might be suspected of murder.

What would happen to them? Would the police believe that they didn't kill Harry? Blythe won't survive in prison. I shouldn't have left her alone in Atlanta. This mess is my fault. I have to make it right.

Step one, getting Blythe away from SAFEPOWER. Step two, getting her away from Carter. Both preyed on her sister's vulnerabilities. Every time she saw Carter's cold, vacant eyes on TV, Sterling's skin crawled.

A female docent with a group of Japanese tourists entered the room, steering the group with her laser pointer to Jean Lafitte's portrait.

Sterling sat down on the padded bench in the center of the room and checked the time on her Cartier watch.

Would Blythe show?

She heard the tourists' murmurs as they 'oohed and aahed' over the magnificent art.

Sterling felt a tap on her shoulder and turned around to find Blythe.

"You came," Sterling said unable to hide her relief.

"I haven't thought about this place in years. We used to have quiet, normal lives, didn't we?" Blythe looked around the room and sat down beside Sterling. The Japanese group moved on to the next hall leaving them alone.

Sterling placed her hand on Blythe's.

"Yes, and it can be that way again. Let me help you. We'll tell the police everything, together. They'll understand."

Blythe pulled her hand away.

"No. They won't understand. We'll be the ones they blame for Harry's death. Besides, it might hurt my SAFEPOWER family. I can't do that to them. They're all I have."

"Blythe, listen. I'm your sister, your blood. SAFEPOWER is NOT your family. I know you want revenge for Christopher's death, but SAFEPOWER's violent protests aren't the answer. And, it's not who you are. They murdered an innocent man last night."

"It wasn't SAFEPOWER's fault," Blythe proclaimed, her voice getting louder. "There were never guards in the past. Besides, Carter said NOW they will take us seriously. We can get Senator Morelli to change the Energy Bill and ensure there won't be any new power lines built." Her voice resonated off the high ceiling in the room.

A security guard walked into the room and asked, "Is there a problem here, ladies?"

"No, sir, just a difference of opinion about the artists. We'll keep it down," Sterling smiled at the guard. Blythe shifted on the bench and played with her locket as the guard left the room.

Sterling lowered her voice, "You were there? Oh no! Blythe, you have to get away from Carter and his evil cult. We once relied on each other for everything and I believe we can do so again. Please place your trust in me instead of a man you've only known a few months. We'll get through this horrible mess together. That's what Christopher would want."

"I don't know. I just don't know. Too much has happened. I'm tired and confused. I can't think straight anymore. I only wanted justice for Christopher's death." Blythe put her head in her hands.

"I understand. I loved him too. He died too young. Let's find out the truth about EMFs and, if they cause cancer, I will stop my industry from building more power lines. I swear on Mom and Dad's memory."

Blythe's eyes focused on her sister's, then widened in fear. Sterling whirled around.

"There you are," Carter Simpson walked up to them and put his hands on Blythe's shoulders.

"Carter, what are you doing here?" Blythe pulled away from him.

"After our unfortunate event last night, I wanted to make sure you were okay. After all, you're my family and family comes first."

"No, I'm her family, and we're having a private conversation." Sterling stood up from the bench. Her 5 ft 10-inch stature towering over Carter's diminutive figure. Carter stepped back and looked up at Sterling.

"So, you must be Blythe's sister, Sterling Barrington. It's so nice to meet you in person. I'm the one who sent you letters about EMF cases."

"You? You sent me those letters?"

"Yes, you needed to know that your industry is killing innocent people. You're in a position of power. You can make a difference. You can stop the killing. Stop the passage of this Energy Bill. Join our cause."

"Your cause? You think violence is the answer. You're a cold-blooded killer. You blow up substations and power lines. How many people have been hurt because you stopped their power? Just think about the hospitals! I would never help you. I am taking my sister with me and, together, we'll unearth the truth."

"Blythe won't leave me. She's one of us now. Isn't that right Blythe? We were there for you in your darkest hour. Not your husband. Not Sterling."

Blythe looked between Sterling and Carter.

"Blythe, let's go. There's nothing left to talk about." Carter offered his hand to her.

"Blythe, you can't go with him. Please, trust me."

"Sterling, he's right. They helped me through my despair. Their way is the only way to get justice for Christopher's death." Blythe took Carter's hand and stood up.

"No, Blythe, it's not justice. It's revenge. Listen to your heart, not your anger," Sterling said.

CHAPTER EIGHTEEN

Detectives Keegan and Angelo returned to the Baltimore Homicide Department after meeting with Sterling. Their desks faced each other. Keegan's was covered with papers, folders, post-it notes, photos of his children and new grandson, Danny. Angelo's desk on the other hand was spotless and had no family photos.

"Damn, we should've brought her in for more questioning. She would've cracked in the box," Keegan pointed at the room with two-way glass. He held the department record for gaining confessions after questioning a suspect in that room and was itching to get another mark in his win column.

"Dan, we didn't have enough to bring her in. She's smart. She's not going to let us ask any more questions unless she's under arrest."

"I know she's guilty. As soon as we get that damn DNA evidence back, we'll nail her to the wall," he pounded his fist on the desk.

"Calm down, Keegan. Your blood pressure is high enough. Don't let some prissy Southern girl get to you. Have patience. We'll get her."

A young man walked up to their desks with a grin on his face. He looked at Detective Angelo as he laid a folder on her desk. "Hey Maria, how're you doing?"

"Fine, Benjy, just fine. You have something for us?"

"Hey Benjy, tell me some good news for a change," Detective Keegan said.

"Achoo."

"Gesundheit? Huh?"

"Someone sneezed on your victim, Brown, after he died. It's not your suspect."

Keegan sat up. "Wait, what did you say? It's not Ms. Barrington's DNA?"

"No, it's not her DNA. But it has similar alleles, so it's someone related to her."

"So, who is it?" Maria said.

"I ran it through CODUS, but neither Ms. Barrington nor her siblings are in the system."

"Damn. So, she didn't do it, but she knows who did, and she's protecting them. Thanks, Benjy. Good work," Detective Angelo said.

"Just doing my job. Hey Maria, want to get a drink after work?"

"Yeah, sure. Meet you at Joe's unless something breaks in this case."

"Ok, I'll see you later."

Benjy left their office and Detective Keegan turned to Maria.

"Well, well, looks like someone has an admirer."

"Shove it, Dan. What's our next step?"

"Do some digging on Ms. Barrington and her family. We have enough ammo to question her again. She'll talk this time."

CHAPTER NINETEEN

Carter took Blythe by the hand. She looked one more time at the Dolley Madison portrait and then at Sterling.

Would she ever see her sister again? Could she desert her last remaining family member?

Carter pulled on her hand. "Come on, Blythe, it's over."

They walked to the SAFEPOWER van in silence. Ever the gentleman, he opened the passenger door for her and helped her up into the vehicle. Blythe put on her seatbelt and stared straight ahead as Carter pulled out of the parking lot.

"Let's go home. The team will make you feel better."

"But, that's not my home. Atlanta. That's my home with my husband and Sterling. What have I done? I ruined my marriage, but I can't lose Sterling. Stop the car. I have to go back to Sterling. I have to make it right. Stop the car!"

"Blythe, calm down. You're not going anywhere. Sterling is the enemy. Can't you see that? She is loyal to an industry that kills kids like Christopher every day. Forget her."

Blythe reached for the door handle and Carter swerved to the nearest curb.

"Stop it! You'll get yourself killed. You're not going back to that evil bitch. You're coming back to the compound with me. We must get ready for our Candlelight Vigil on the Mall. It's our best chance to prove to the country that we are on the side of peace."

"I don't want to be a part of SAFEPOWER anymore. Please, just let me out."

"No. You signed on to be a part of our family. You're not leaving. If you can't shape up and help with our plans, then there will be consequences. We've worked too hard and come too far to stop this Energy Bill and the killing of innocent victims. I'm not going to disappoint him or our followers. Now shut up and stay put."

"Him? Who's him? Who are you talking about?"

"No one. Just an ardent supporter who wishes to remain anonymous. He's helped us financially. I'm not going to let him down."

"I'm sorry, Carter. I'll help. I'm upset, but I'll get over it. You're right. We have to stop the Energy Bill from passing. No other children deserve to die."

CHAPTER TWENTY

Sterling took another sip of coffee from her Emory mug. She had tossed and turned all night after her failed meeting with Blythe.

Why did Blythe leave with Carter? Would they ever speak again, much less see each other?

She tried to focus on work, but her thoughts were on Blythe. Toni walked into her office. The gold bracelets on her arm jingled when she handed her some papers.

"Anything you want me to do?"

She sat down in one of Sterling's chairs. Her purple leather pants squeaked as she crossed her legs.

"Um, what did you say?"

"Earth to Sterling. What's wrong with you? Tonight's the big rally of the wacko environmentalists. Duh, the ones who say we're killing people."

"Oh yes, of course. I've got a lot on my mind. I'm working on some new press releases. We've done all we can do."

Toni shrugged and left her office. Sterling turned back to her computer. A moment later she heard a noise and, without looking toward the door, said "Toni, did you need something else?"

"No, Ms. Barrington, it's Detectives Keegan and Angelo. We need to speak with you again," Detective Keegan said. The officers stood in front of Sterling's desk.

She whirled around to face the uninvited guests. "Officers, I didn't know you were coming today. I'm very busy right now. Your questions will have to wait until tomorrow."

"We showed ourselves in. This can't wait. Besides, you'll be interested in what we have to say. We got the DNA results back for the unknown substance on Harry's face. It turns out someone sneezed on him. Someone related to you."

"What? What about the skin from Raven's paw? I'm sure it's from Harry's killer. Did you get those lab results?"

"No, not yet. Besides, we may not need them. Who're you covering for, Ms. Barrington? It's only a matter of time until we find out who killed Harry. If you refuse to talk to us, we can charge you with murder."

"Detectives, as I told you yesterday, unless you're going to arrest me, then I have nothing more to say. Please see yourself out."

"Don't be a fool, Ms. Barrington. Give us a name or go to prison yourself." Detective Keegan looked over at Detective Angelo and nodded.

"We can place you at the scene and we found your business card there. We know you went to his home before the murder and you have motive. Tell us what Harry had on your industry. It must have been something big. Big enough for you to shut him up forever."

"You're wrong, Detective. I wanted to help Harry, not kill him."

"One last chance, Ms. Barrington. Who're you covering for?"

"I'm not saying another word without a lawyer."

"Ok, you had your chance. Detective Angelo, read Ms. Barrington her rights."

Detective Angelo pulled out her handcuffs and walked over to Sterling. "Turn around Ms. Barrington and put your hands behind your back. You are under arrest for the murder of Harry Brown."

Detective Angelo read Sterling the Miranda rights.

"Do you understand these rights, Ms. Barrington?" Detective Angelo closed the cuffs around Sterling's wrists.

"Yes. I understand. You're making a terrible mistake." Sterling bent down to pick up her bag.

"I'll take that Ms. Barrington." Detective Keegan took Sterling's purse from her bound hands. "Maybe spending some time in our cooler will make you talk. Lead the way, Maria."

Detective Angelo took Sterling by the arm into the hallway. Several staffers stood in their doorways to watch the procession, judging her.

Toni stood up and said, "Sterling, are you going to jail?"

"Toni, call Trevor, tell him to meet me at the Baltimore Police Headquarters. Just do it."

"Ok, ok, I'll call him now," Toni said.

"Come on, Ms. Barrington. We don't have time for chit chat."

The detectives escorted her to the elevator. As the door began to close, she saw Sandy in the lobby sporting a Cheshire Cat smile.

CHAPTER TWENTY-ONE

Sandy followed the man and woman down the hall as he walked toward his office. He hadn't given them much thought until they turned into Sterling's office. That piqued his curiosity.

He stood outside Sterling's office and pretended to look through a file on Toni's desk. Toni looked up at him and said, "Need something Sandy?"

"No, shush. Who are those people in Sterling's office?"

"That's those Baltimore detectives. I guess they have more questions for Sterling."

"Shit. They're back?"

He didn't have to strain to hear the exchange because the male detective spoke in a very loud and threatening voice. From what he could hear, they didn't know anything about him or that he went to Harry's. Then the pièce de résistance, they arrested her.

He stepped back into an empty office so Sterling couldn't see him when they walked her out. Her hands were cuffed, and she told Toni to call that damn boyfriend of hers. The officers took her to the elevator and he followed. He wanted her to know that he was watching, to know her shame. She glared at him before the doors closed.

I couldn't have planned this better myself. The police believe Sterling and some relative killed Harry.

He went back to Toni's desk and said, "Have you called Congressman Reese yet?"

"Yeah, I just got his assistant. He's in an Energy Committee meeting, and she'll get him a note about Sterling. Sheesh, Sterling's a murderer?"

"I guess we're all capable of committing horrific acts if the need arises."

"Damn, Sandy. I hope I don't get on your bad side. You scare me."

"Where's Walker? I need to update him on this situation."

"He's back in his office. He should be off his conference call with the PAC members."

Sandy strutted down the hall to Walker's office, tapped on the door frame and entered.

Walker looked up from his papers.

"What's going on out there? I heard a commotion during my conference call."

"You'll never belie.."

"By the way, have you seen Bob today? I need to talk to him about some numbers that don't look right on the PAC donations."

"Bob? I, I don't know. Why would I know?" Sandy said.

"Because you two are drinking buddies, that's why. Now, what did you come in here for?"

"I've got big news," Sandy beamed at him, shut the door and sat in one of the arm chairs. He put his feet up on Walker's desk and said, "This is a great day."

Walker leaned across the desk and pushed Sandy's feet off. "Keep your fucking feet off my desk. What are you talking about? Did you find Brown's notes?"

"No, no, this is even better. Sterling got arrested for Harry's murder."

"Holy Shit. Fill me in on the details."

"Those Baltimore dicks came back today. They said they have DNA evidence that's from someone related to Sterling, like a sibling or something. The police think Sterling's covering for this person.

They intimated Sterling's an accomplice or at least an accessory to Harry's murder."

"Oh my God. I've never heard her talk about any family, but I can access The Franklin personnel records. Let's see who Sterling is protecting."

Walker typed a few strokes and Sterling Barrington's file appeared.

"Here it is: Sterling Barrington, parents deceased, sister Blythe Corbin of Atlanta. I've heard that name. Oh my God, the SAFEPOWER spokeswoman! Sterling's a spy. She's working against the industry. We've got to get Harry's notes back from her or she'll destroy us."

"Walker, do you think Sterling gave her sister Harry's notes?" Sandy said.

"Ok, let's think a minute. If she had given Blythe the evidence, the SAFEPOWER group wouldn't have sat on it. They would have released it since the Energy Bill vote is only a few days away. That would have been their ace in the hole. So, Sterling must have hidden Harry's notes. That's it. Tonight, we find those fucking notes and stop this mess. Sterling will still be in the Baltimore Jail, so we won't be bothered. We'll meet here at 7:00 pm, search her office, and then go to her apartment if we haven't found them. This bitch won't ruin my life or my industry."

CHAPTER TWENTY-TWO

Sterling rode in the cracked, stained backseat of the tan sedan in silence. She struggled to sit comfortably with her hands cuffed.

I can get through this…for Blythe.

The two detectives sat in the front seat, partition between them and Sterling, dispatch radio spouting garbled, undistinguishable voices. It reminded Sterling of metro train conductors. Passengers never knew what they were saying.

She watched the DC landmarks pass as Detective Keegan drove to HQ and Detective Angelo sifted through papers. She prayed Toni reached Trevor. He'd be shocked but would understand after she explained everything to him.

When they arrived at Baltimore Police Headquarters, Sterling was subjected to the humiliating process of being searched, photographed and fingerprinted, then she was put in a holding cell.

"You'll be in here until your bail hearing," Detective Angelo said.

"When will that be, and when do I get my phone call?" Sterling clutched the bars on the door.

"There's a waiting line for the phone so it may be awhile. Just be quiet and sit down like a good girl."

Sterling turned around and surveyed the cell. A built-in bench ran around the puke green walls. A middle-aged black woman sat on one corner with her head against the wall, snoring. A pungent stench came from the other corner, where she saw a bolted down toilet and a sink.

She sat close to the cell door and rubbed her wrists. They were red and chapped from the tight cuffs.

Who else wanted Harry dead? Who knew he had information that could destroy the power industry? It had to be someone who knew Harry. Someone who worked with him. Walker? He's been in the industry a long time. He could've known Harry. Walker and Senator Morelli need the energy bill passed to get more power lines. That would ensure success for both their careers. Plus, Walker's power hungry. If Morelli became President, Walker could end up as Secretary of Energy. Would they have killed for that? Power is a strong drug. The thought of them losing it may have been too much. If Harry wanted to publicize the truth about a cover-up in the industry, then they would want him stopped. But did Walker do the deed? No,

Walker's been out of it lately. Who else? Who were Walker's bloodhounds? Sandy. It had to be Sandy. He'd do anything for Walker. He must have followed me the first time I went to Harry's. He killed Harry then tore the house apart to find Harry's evidence that power lines kill. No doubt he gave it to Walker. I have to get that evidence back and make it public. The Energy Bill cannot pass.

"OK, time for your hearing," a female officer said as the cell door pulled open.

"I need to call my attorney. I can't go in there without my lawyer."

"Well, then it's your lucky day. Your lawyer's here, waiting in the court room," the officer said.

"When's it my turn, Smitty?" Sterling's cell mate asked.

"In due time, Sheniqua. In due time."

The officer re-cuffed Sterling, this time with her wrists in front, and led her down the hall to the courtroom.

"Be quiet and sit down in this section. Stand up, when your name's called."

Sterling nodded, slid into the row of seats and sat down.

Across the courtroom, she saw Trevor. He nodded and smiled at her.

For the first time in days, she felt hope.

After processing multiple cases, the court bailiff finally said,

"Ms. Sterling Barrington, case number 5987."

Sterling walked to the end of the row and an officer escorted

her to the table where Trevor stood.

"Ms. Barrington, you are charged with first degree murder of

Mr. Harry Brown of Baltimore. How do you plead?" said the judge,

an older woman with gray hair, a wrinkled face and hoarse voice.

Trevor looked over at Sterling, "Go ahead, Sterling."

"Not guilty, your honor."

"Your honor, the state requests Ms. Barrington be remanded to

jail because she is a flight risk," the assistant district attorney, Bill

Green, said.

"Your honor, Trevor Reese, representing the defendant. I'm

requesting that Ms. Barrington be released on her own recognizance

with no bail. This is her first offense. She will relinquish her passport

and I can vouch that she will not be a flight risk."

"Mr. Reese, or should I say Congressman Reese, are you slumming today?" the judge said.

"No, your honor, just keeping up my practice."

"Bail will be set at $500,000. Trial will be in 3 weeks," the judge banged her gavel.

"Next case bailiff."

Sterling hugged Trevor. "Thank you for helping me."

"I've got the bail money ready. Go with the officer and I'll see you in a few minutes," Trevor said.

An hour passed before they released Sterling from the holding cell.

She took a deep breath of the steamy air outside the station.

Tom smiled and opened the back door of Trevor's car for her.

"Tom, back to DC please," Trevor said.

"Yes, sir."

"What an awful experience. How can I ever thank you?" Sterling said.

"You can start by telling me what's going on," Trevor reached over and rubbed her neck.

"Here goes."

When she finished her story, Trevor said, "my God, Sterling, what a horrible few days. I'll take you home, so you can rest."

"No, not yet. I'd love to take a shower and scrub the jailhouse off, but I've got to take care of some business tonight. First, I have to go to The Franklin and get my notes on EMFs. I also want to search Walker's and Sandy's offices to look for Harry's notes. And, I've got to find Blythe. SAFEPOWER's holding their rally tonight on the Mall. I'll drag her kicking and screaming away from Carter if I have to. That man is evil."

"I'm going with you."

"Thanks, Trevor. I could use the help."

"Sterling, do you think Blythe knows who killed Harry?"

"I don't know, but I believe she knows something that she's not telling me."

Trevor's cell phone rang and interrupted their conversation.

"Let me see who this is. Just a minute," Trevor pulled his cell phone out and looked at the caller ID. The phone continued to buzz. "It's Senator Morelli. Let me see what he wants. Hello, Reese here. Well, hello Senator Morelli. To what do I owe this call? Tonight? This can't wait until tomorrow? I'm out of the district right now so

I'll have to meet you in two hours at your office. Yes, I'll see you then."

Trevor ended his call and turned to Sterling, "Senator Morelli said he must see me tonight to discuss the Energy Bill."

"The same day I tell you about Harry and EMFs, Senator Morelli wants to meet with you. I don't believe in coincidence, Trevor. He must be in on the cover-up."

"That's why I agreed to meet with him. To hear what he wants to say. Sterling, do you still have your tape recorder with you? I'd like to use it during my conversation with the Senator."

"Yes, here it is," Sterling retrieved the tape recorder from her bag.

"Now that I'm meeting with Morelli, I can't go with you to The Franklin."

"I'll be fine, Trevor."

"I'm going to have Tom come back for you after he drops me off and take you to the Mall to look for Blythe. Tom, after Ms. Barrington finds her sister, drive them to her apartment and stay with them until I call."

"Yes, sir," Tom said.

The lights of DC shone as they neared the District on New

York Avenue.

Blythe, I promise you. We'll be a family again.

CHAPTER TWENTY-THREE

Located halfway between the Hill and the White House on the corner of Seventh Street and Pennsylvania Avenue, The Franklin Energy Institute was the main tenant on the Navy Memorial plaza. The FBI and the National Archives buildings sat across the street with an orange Metro stop nearby. The plaza's half-moon shape, tall columns and spraying fountains fit in with classic DC architecture, even though it opened in 1987.

Trevor's Lincoln pulled to the curb of The Franklin. Through the tinted car windows Sterling saw a large crowd on the plaza in front of the building. Its prime location attracted tourists year-round.

"Sterling, I'll see you later. Good luck with everything."

"Thanks. I can't wait to hear what the Senator wanted."

She kissed Trevor, exited the car and looked at the crowd of people. These were not the usual tourist types that frequented the area. They were vocal and boisterous, carrying signs, banners and wearing buttons with anti-EMF slogans. They chanted, "Down with The Franklin."

These people are here for SAFEPOWER.

They heckled her as she pushed through the crowd to the front entrance.

They think I'm the enemy.

She took the elevator to her floor and wound her way around the quiet hallway. A few office lights beamed from open doors like spotlights on a stage. She walked through darkness, then light, darkness, then light.

First, she would retrieve her EMF documents, then search Walker's and Sandy's offices. She needed evidence that proved they knew EMFs kill and that they murdered Harry. After that, she would go to the Mall, find Blythe, and clear their names.

She downloaded her desk computer documents to a flash drive and deleted all her files. Next, she filled her bag with her handwritten notes, folders and books. She looked around her office one more time.

Where's the article on the EMF study in Europe? I left it in the library. Need to search the other offices before heading there.

Walker's office was a dirty joke. It appeared he kept every piece of paper he ever read. This would be more difficult than she thought.

She opened drawers, rifled through file cabinets and looked in book shelves. She found nothing that tied him to Harry. Most of his cache held old, unimportant memos. She squatted down by the bottom drawer of his desk and pulled on the handle. It wouldn't budge. She searched the desk for something to help her open the drawer. Sticking out from under the desk pad, she spied a silver letter opener, grabbed it and pried open the lock. Under a false bottom, she found Walker's secrets; a bottle of Vodka and a pack of cigarettes, but no evidence.

Sterling went across the hall to Sandy's office, which was the complete opposite of Walker's. Everything was labeled and organized. She couldn't find anything to link him to Harry either.

Damn. I know they killed Harry. Where did they hide Harry's evidence?

****

Sandy and Walker met outside The Franklin.

"Shit. Look at all those liberal loonies here protesting our industry. Let's get those notes and get out of here," Sandy said.

"Damn weirdos. Why don't they get a life and leave us alone?" Walker yelled to the protesters as he walked to the door.

"Sandy, go up to Sterling's office and start the search. I've got to make a stop first. I'll meet you up there in a bit."

Walker swiped his employee card and entered the dark company library. He left the lights off and walked to a separate rectangular glass room in the back.

Built like a greenhouse, it had museum quality lighting and special air equipment to preserve the world's largest collection of Ben Franklin's artifacts, papers and personal effects.

The state-of-the-art security system didn't deter Walker. He'd gotten the code by seducing the librarian. He punched in the four digits and entered the room.

****

Sterling left Sandy's office and walked down the four flights of interior stairs to the library.

****

Sandy exited the elevator and entered the marketing department, heading for Sterling's office.

****

Sterling entered the library and felt for the light switch on the wall. She heard a noise and stopped. She tiptoed in the darkness to the middle of the library. The Ben Franklin archives glowed.

Sterling inched her way toward the archives, taking cover behind thick periodicals. She was about 10 feet away when she saw Walker.

What's he doing here?

Walker knelt behind a glass case of Ben Franklin's personal effects. He opened the sliding doors of the case and reached inside for one of the objects. Walker removed a humidor and pulled something out that Sterling could not see. He smiled, put the object back in the humidor and returned it to the case. He stood up and stretched, looking extremely relieved.

Sterling crept back to the opposite end of the bookshelf and stood with her back up against the shelf, facing away from the archives and Walker. She heard Walker go to the library door, open it and slam it shut.

Sweat beaded on her forehead as she waited.

Would Walker return? I've got to find out what he hid. How can I get in there?

She went to the door and looked at the security key pad. There were no lights. She took hold of the door handle and found the door ajar. Walker forgot to shut it and reset the alarm.

She stepped inside the room filled with historical objects and looked around. She'd never been in here. Only the librarian had access to the archives, and now Walker apparently. Ben Franklin had touched every item. If only she could take her time and look at each piece. No time. She went directly to the glass case, pulled out the ornately carved box and lifted the lid. Musty, stagnant air filled her nostrils. Inside she found several disks.

This must be Harry's evidence about EMFs.

She took the disks, put the humidor back in the case and closed it. Sterling left the archives and made sure the door closed. She rushed over to one of the library computers to view the disks' contents. The computer was locked and required a password. She checked her watch. Tom wouldn't arrive for a while. She could go back to her office and use that computer.

A few steps from her office, Sterling heard voices.

"I can't find any of her notes, Walker. She must have them with her," Sandy said.

"Shit. We have to find them and keep her mouth shut," Walker said.

Sandy's with Walker?

She turned around to leave and bumped the wastebasket at Toni's desk. It crashed into the cubicle wall. She clutched her bag and ran out of the department to the elevators.

"Shit. Sandy, see what happened," Walker said.

Sandy left Sterling's office, looked around the department and found no one. He walked to the floor lobby where he saw the elevator doors close with Sterling inside.

"Get back here you bitch," Sandy said.

Sandy banged on the closed elevator doors as Walker rushed over.

"Who got on the elevator?"

"Sterling."

"Don't just stand there shithead, take the stairs and find her. Call me on my cell when you get her."

On the first floor, Sterling flew out the door onto the crowded plaza. She worked her way through the protesters to the curb.

I hope Tom's here.

She turned around and saw Sandy exit the building. She whirled around and headed toward the Metro.

****

Sandy spotted her on the Metro's down escalator.

"Come back here you bitch."

Some of the protestors looked at him as he followed her down to the station.

****

Sterling pulled out her transit card and waited as out-of-towners fumbled with their tickets. She worked her way to the middle of the noisy platform and stood on tiptoe to look over the mob. She spied Sandy on his way down, his eyes darting around.

She took an Atlanta Braves cap out of her bag, twisted her long hair into a knot and shoved it under the cap. A horn sounded and a train pulled into the station with a whoosh of air. The doors opened and people spilled out of the train onto the platform.

Sterling tried to move forward to get on the train but got caught up in the swarm exiting the station. On the up escalator, she craned her neck and saw Sandy step on the train.

Back on the plaza street level, she ran toward the curb. She took off the cap and her long red hair spilled out. She waved at Tom, who stood by the car, ran through the protesters and climbed in the back seat.

"Are you all right Miss?" Tom said as he started the car.

"I am now. Please drive to the Mall. I've got to rescue Blythe."

CHAPTER TWENTY-FOUR

Tom dropped Trevor outside the Longworth House office building.

"Have Sterling call me when you pick her up."

"Yes, sir. Have a good meeting."

He walked up the marble steps of the historic building where former and present lawmakers made deals, wrote landmark bills and wielded power.

What does Morelli want with me tonight? I should be with Sterling.

He said hello to the security detail and went through the metal detector, then made his way to the Senator's large office, a definite Senate tenure perk.

Even at this late hour, an older professionally dressed woman worked at a desk in the reception area. An open door behind her allowed Trevor to see the Senator's young, eager interns and staffers also hard at work.

"Trevor Reese for the Senator," Trevor said to the woman.

"Yes, Congressman, please have a seat and I'll let the Senator know you're here. May I get you a beverage?"

"No, thank you."

She walked across the reception area and tapped on the Senator's private office door, walked in, and shut the door behind her. Trevor sat down on an upholstered club chair and looked around the reception area filled with certificates of honor and photographs of the Senator with luminaries from his numerous years in office.

Trevor reached into his suit coat pocket, switched on Sterling's tape recorder and put his cell phone on silent.

The secretary came out of the Senator's chambers and sat behind her desk. A few moments later, her phone rang.

"Yes, Senator, I'll tell him."

She hung up the phone and looked over at Trevor. "You may go in now, Congressman."

"Thank you."

He stood up, straightened his jacket and tie, and walked into an office that belonged in the pages of Architectural Digest. The room was elegantly furnished with Persian rugs, Tiffany lamps and hunting trophies. A large, carved mahogany desk sat in front of windows facing the lit Capitol.

The Senator stood up and walked around to shake Trevor's hand with a tight, menacing grip.

If you want a pissing contest, Senator, that's fine with me.

Trevor smiled and squeezed back with fervor.

"Glad you could stop by, Congressman. We've got a problem we need to handle, right now."

The Senator sat in a wingback tapestry chair and gestured for Trevor to sit on a tufted navy leather couch across from him.

He lit a Cuban cigar and took a few puffs. "Would you care for one, Congressman?"

"No, thank you, Senator. I don't smoke. What is the urgent matter you wish to discuss?"

"Your vote on the Energy Bill."

"I'm going to vote against it, Senator. It's not the right bill for the country."

"For a freshman congressman, you've made your point and done a good job for your people. But now is the time to get on the right side of this bill, my side. As Chairman of the committee, I'm setting the vote for next week."

"Next week? Do you believe you have enough votes for the Energy Bill to pass?"

"With your vote, yes, we will have enough votes."

"Senator, this requires more discussion. Some new information about EMFs has become available that will drastically impact the current bill. It is my duty to investigate and determine the validity of said information. If the electric industry is indeed concealing the truth about power line safety, I can't vote for this bill."

"I see," said the Senator, taking a long puff on his cigar and discarding it in a Waterford Crystal ash tray. "Did you get this information from Ms. Barrington?"

"Yes, she believes there is an industry cover-up concerning power line safety, and I agree with her."

"Bullshit. Just because you're banging her doesn't mean she's right. That old whistle blower gave her false information. If Brown really knew the truth, why wait until now to reveal it?"

"I didn't tell you who gave Sterling the information. What ties do you have to Harry Brown?"

"That troublemaker has been causing problems for decades. I presumed Brown gave her the false information."

"I didn't know the man, but he must have had his reasons. We need to go through his documents to see why he felt this way. The vote cannot be set yet."

"What documents? Where are they? Does Ms. Barrington have them?"

"She's retrieving them as we speak."

"Hmm. Interesting. I heard Ms. Barrington would be spending the night in the Baltimore jail for Harry's murder."

"I don't know where you're getting your information, but she's innocent and she's out on bail."

"I don't believe there are any documents to retrieve. The vote will be next week, and you will vote for it. I can't and won't allow my constituents to go through another blackout. More plants, transmission towers and lines must be built."

"Then, I will make it my mission to stop the vote and find out the truth about power lines and the EMFs they emit."

The Senator looked at Trevor, picked up his cigar and blew three rings of smoke that wafted over the Congressman.

"It is my job to get this bill through and that's what I am going to do, whether you like it or not. You haven't been up here long. I can and will make your political life miserable. You will stop Ms. Barrington from publishing the EMFs information and vote for the bill."

"Is that a threat, Senator? No one threatens me. This meeting is over."

Trevor shut the office door and the Senator laid his cigar down, pushed the intercom to his secretary and said, "Get me Walker Nelson, now."

Power Lies | J.L. Phillips

CHAPTER TWENTY-FIVE

Walker stood outside The Franklin on the plaza. He scanned the crowd for Sterling and Sandy.

Where the fuck did they go?

He called Sandy's cell again. Still no answer. He crushed his cigarette under his foot and was lighting a new one when he saw someone run out of the Metro escalator. The person took off a baseball cap and long hair flowed out.

There's the bitch.

Sterling crossed the plaza, got into a black Lincoln and sped away.

Damn. That must be Reese's car. Shit, shit, shit.

He punched in Senator Morelli's cell number.

"I'm at the office. Brown's notes aren't in her office. The bitch is out of jail and she knows we're on to her. What do you want to do?"

"Shit, just what we need, more problems. I just finished with Reese. He's trouble, just like his girlfriend. He's going to help her unearth the truth about EMFs and stop the Energy Bill."

"Fuck. Do you want me to handle him?"

"No. This debacle is your fault. You hired the woman. Stay put. I'm sending Vinnie over to get you. Go to her apartment and find those damn notes or else."

"Yeah, yeah. I know what to do. Quit treating me like one of your flunkies. It's not just your neck on the fucking line."

"Just get the evidence and silence the noise."

CHAPTER TWENTY-SIX

The Lincoln crept along Pennsylvania Avenue in heavy traffic toward the Mall. Sterling was trying to catch her breath after the wild Metro chase. She grabbed a water bottle from the small ice chest in the back of the car, lifted her hair, and pressed the cool bottle against the back of her neck.

"Miss, the Congressman asked me to have you call him," Tom said.

"Thanks, Tom."

Trevor's cell phone went to voicemail.

"Hi, it's me. I got my notes, but Sandy and Walker know. I'll fill you in on the details later. We're on our way to get Blythe, then to my apartment. Call me when your meeting is over."

Ahead, she could see the Mall aglow. Hundreds of people holding candles overhead faced a stage in front of the Lincoln monument. A female pop star serenaded the swaying crowd.

"Tom, park down by the monument. Blythe will be with Carter and I'm sure he's near the stage."

"Yes, Miss."

Tom pulled up to an open spot by the curb. Trevor's congressional plates allowed them to park in a no parking zone.

"Thanks, Tom. Please wait here. I'm going to get my sister out of this nightmare."

Sterling pushed through the crowd toward the stage. Along the way, she rejected candles and signs from volunteers. She saw several notable environmentalists and vocal left-wing actors on the stage. A man stepped up to the microphone and a hush fell over the crowd. Carter raised his hands to silence the crowd.

I've got to find Blythe before he's finished.

"Thank you, thank you, dear friends and SAFEPOWER supporters. We're so glad you're here for this memorial service honoring victims of EMFs. The electric industry and right-wing politicians don't believe the EMFs produced by power lines kill. They want more power lines, more transmission towers, more deaths. The Energy Bill would allow this to happen. This bill must not pass," Carter said.

The crowd chanted, "No more power lines."

Carter quieted the crowd and continued his speech. Sterling didn't see Blythe on the stage or in the audience around it, so she walked behind the stage.

Spotlights illuminated the area, with several behind-the-scenes staff guarding the stage and checking the sound. A small Medusa-like trailer with numerous cables and cords snaking out of it was nearby. The door opened, and Blythe walked over to the stage, watching Carter.

Sterling used cloaked areas to carefully approach her sister. Once close enough, she grabbed Blythe by the arm and pulled her back into the shadows away from the stage.

"Sterling? What are you doing here?"

"Blythe, you've got to come with me."

Blythe whirled around and yanked her arm from Sterling's grip.

"I can't come with you. Carter will be furious if he sees you."

"You mean he'll kill me like he did the station guard?"

"No, no. We didn't know they had a guard."

"Blythe, the police are onto you. I spent the afternoon in jail as an accomplice to Harry's murder. I'm here to help you."

"Arrested? Oh my gosh!"

"Blythe, this is serious. We must leave right now. I found Harry's evidence and there are some guys who want it back, badly."

"What do you mean you have Harry's evidence?" Blythe grasped her locket and held it tight.

"I'll tell you later, but we have to go before Carter finishes his speech."

Carter's voice got louder. He sounded like a television evangelist giving a sermon. The sisters looked toward the stage.

"We have the power to stop the Energy Bill. With your help, it shall not pass. When you leave tonight, you will be handed a letter to send to your state leaders. This letter asks them to vote no on the Energy Bill. Let's join hands and sing, We Shall Overcome."

The crowd moved closer together to begin the song.

"Blythe, if you don't leave with me now, I won't be able to protect you. You've got to trust me."

"You're right. You always have been. I'll go with you."

"Thank you for trusting me. Follow me."

Sterling took Blythe's hand and led her through the crowd to the car.

****

Carter finished his speech and walked off stage. A crew member gave him some water and a towel. He wiped his face and wet the towel, slinging it around his neck.

"Great job, Carter," one of the stage hands yelled to him. He smiled and accepted congratulations from a few other SAFEPOWER team members.

"You did it, Carter. There's thousands of supporters here tonight. The Energy Bill will never pass," Mike said, patting Carter on the back. Carter nodded and looked around.

"Where's Blythe?" he asked Mike.

"I saw her a minute ago talking to some redhead."

"A redhead? Oh shit. We've got to find her. You two, get a

group together and search the crowd. If Blythe's gone,

SAFEPOWER's dead."

CHAPTER TWENTY-SEVEN

The black Escalade pulled up to the front of The Franklin plaza. Walker took one last drag from his cigarette and clumsily climbed into the passenger seat. "So, where's the bitch's apartment?" Vinnie inquired.

"Crap, why is this SUV so fucking hard to get into."

"You're just old. Now where are we going?"

"Arlington. Courthouse Road. The high rise there."

"You sure she won't be there?"

"Naw. And if she happens to show up, we'll take care of her."

Vinnie drove to Sterling's high rise in short order and parked on a side street. The two men got out and walked toward the service entrance.

"Why aren't we going in the front?" Walker said.

"Because there's a concierge in front who would remember seeing us if the police question him and definitely a camera. There's always a door unlocked in the back though and these expensive residences are too cheap to put a camera on the service entrance. Wait here a minute and I'll find an entry point."

"Ok. Make it quick," Walker lit a new cigarette and leaned against the brick wall.

Vinnie returned and said, "Just what I thought, no guard. Follow me."

The two men entered the building through an unlocked door in the delivery area. To their left sat a wooden desk laden with clipboards that read pool, laundry, vending machines. Across from the desk was the service elevator.

Vinnie pushed the up button and turned to Walker, "What's her apartment number?"

"Oh, shit. I don't know."

"What the fuck?"

"Fuck you. I forgot to get it."

"Ok, let me look around, there's got to be a master key or something down here. Well, well. It's your lucky day. Look over there."

On a back wall, opposite the service elevator, hung a corkboard filled with names, unit numbers and keys.

"Jackpot. Barrington, 538. At least she's the only Barrington, ya jackass."

"Shut up, Vinnie."

The service elevator creaked and clanged on their ride up.

"Shit. I hope no one comes to check out who's on the freight elevator

this late," Walker said.

They walked onto an empty fifth floor hallway, the luxurious,

soft carpet masking their footsteps. Vinnie pulled out the key.

"Ready?"

"What about an alarm? We don't have a code."

"Shit, Walker. These places never have alarms because they

have a concierge downstairs to keep unwanted guests out."

"Ok, you take the right side of the apartment, and I'll take the

left. Then, we'll search the common areas together. Go through

everything. Harry's notes have got to be here. That bitch isn't going

to ruin our plans," Walker said.

CHAPTER TWENTY-EIGHT

Tom pulled away from the Mall and the SAFEPOWER rally with Sterling and Blythe in the backseat.

"Thank you, Blythe," said Sterling, hugging her sister.

"I'm the one who should thank you. I hope you'll forgive me. I have something important to tell you," she nodded her head toward Tom and whispered "Alone."

"Of course, I forgive you. Let's talk when we get to my apartment. Now, we have all the time in the world."

They crossed over the Key Bridge and Sterling said, "There's my building, Blythe. We're almost there."

At last she had her family back. After she and Blythe visited, she would go through the disks she found in The Franklin library. Then she would ensure the public knew the truth about power lines and how their EMFs cause illnesses and deaths.

As the car approached her building, Tom asked, "Where should I park, Miss?"

"The underground parking. They have guest spaces. Turn down that ramp."

"Yes, Miss."

The garage held numerous cars, but no people. The three rode up the resident elevator in silence. Sterling unlocked her door and showed the two in.

"Come in, come in. Blythe, I'll make you some tea, then we can talk. Tom, would you like anything?"

"No ma'am."

She turned into the kitchen and set her bag on the counter.

"Raven, Raven. Here kitty, kitty."

"Who's Raven?" Blythe asked.

"My new cat. I brought her from Harry's."

"Miss, stay back. I think you've been robbed."

Sterling looked toward the living room in front of her and saw couch cushions thrown to the floor, curtains pulled down from their rods and end tables overturned.

"Tom, please call the police. I'll call Trevor again. Blythe, have a seat at the dining room table while we figure this out."

She gestured to the table between the kitchen and living room. Tom walked over to the kitchen phone and Sterling pulled out her cell phone, pushing shortcut number three for Trevor's cell.

"Miss, the phone's dead," Tom said.

"Drop the phone, Sterling. You too old man."

Walker stepped into the living room from Sterling's bedroom, holding a gun. Her gun.

"Walker, please lower the gun. No one here is a threat to you," she said calmly, laying her phone on the dining room table.

"Don't play stupid, Sterling. You are the threat. I want Harry's notes, NOW. I know you took them."

"That's why you're here? Pointing my gun at me? Those notes will end your career, won't they? I'll never give them to you. The truth will come out, Walker, and I'll make sure of it."

"No, you won't, you bitch," Walker said, moving closer to her and shoving the gun in her face.

"Get away from her," Tom yelled, lunging toward Walker with a taser.

Walker pulled the trigger and Tom fell to the floor clutching his chest. Blythe screamed and Sterling ran over to Tom, kneeling beside him.

"Tom? Tom? Walker, you killed him. You are a monster."
Sterling looked up at Walker. His gun smoked as blood flowed out of Tom's chest wound.

"Move away from him, Sterling." Walker waved the gun at her as Vinnie ran into the living room.

"Shit, what did you do?" Vinnie looked at Sterling, Blythe and Tom's lifeless body.

"Collateral damage. Get back to work," Walker said carelessly.

Sterling walked over to Blythe and put an arm around her. She was shaking and blocking the carnage with her hands.

"Sterling, who is that?" Blythe whispered.

"My boss."

"Ok, stop the chit chat girls and move over to the couch. Vinnie, keep looking for the damn notes."

"We need to get out of here. Someone had to hear the shot," Vinnie said.

"Naw. This expensive building has thick walls and no one's going to check on Sterling. No one in this town cares about her. Now, get back to work already!"

Vinnie shrugged his shoulders and walked out of the room.

"That's Senator Morelli's aide isn't it? If he's helping you, then the Senator must be in on the cover up too. It all makes sense. He wants the Energy Bill to pass so he's keeping the truth hidden by any means necessary. Did he order you to murder Harry, Walker?"

"Shut up, Sterling. I'm trying to decide how to make your death look like a family quarrel gone wrong. Why don't I just shoot your sister then you and put your gun in your dead hand?"

Not shaken by his plotting, Sterling continued to hound him, "How long have concealed the truth, Walker? How long have you known that power lines create EMFs and cause cancer? Innocent people have died."

"I've known for decades. Decades, you hear me? So did Harry. We were on the same research team, sworn to secrecy. I kept my mouth shut, but Harry didn't. Traitors deserve to die."

"Harry was a valiant man who wanted to do the right thing. To stop the lies and the murders!"

"Shut up, you ignorant cow. It's business, the way of the world. Nothing will ever change. Power lines will continue to multiply because finding an alternative would cost too much. I didn't let Harry ruin my life or my industry, and I'm not going to let you or your liberal sister."

"Christopher, my sweet Christopher," Blythe said as tears streamed down her face.

"Who the fuck is Christopher?" Walker said.

"My son. The power lines behind our house killed him. It's your fault."

"Blythe, stop."

Vinnie came back into the living room, clearly angry. He walked over to Sterling and put a gun against her temple. "Ok, lady, enough of this crap. Where are the notes? Tell me now or you both die."

Blythe jumped up and grabbed Vinnie's arm, trying to redirect the gun. Walker fired at Blythe and missed, hitting Vinnie in the neck. Vinnie fell backwards while pulling the trigger and hit Blythe in the chest. The bullet exited Blythe's back and hit Sterling in the shoulder. Sterling cried out, "NO," as Blythe dropped to the floor.

Sterling knelt beside her sister, putting pressure on the wound. Blythe's body shook. There was so much blood.

Walker crossed the room and stood over them, gun aimed at Sterling's forehead.

"One last chance, Sterling. Where are Harry's notes?"

Blythe grabbed Walker's leg and bit into his ankle with intensity. He cursed and dropped the gun while trying to kick Blythe. Sterling quickly retrieved it, amazed at her sister's tenacity, and pointed it at Walker.

"It's over, Walker."

"It's not over, Sterling. You'll have to kill me and we both know you can't."

She pulled the trigger. The empty chamber clicked. She kept pulling the trigger, praying there was another bullet, but nothing happened. Walker limped to the door.

"You won't get away with this!"

"Yes, Sterling, I will."

CHAPTER TWENTY-NINE

Trevor stormed out of Senator Morelli's office. He loosened his tie and pushed the down button on the Representatives Only elevator but decided not to wait for the antique brass carriage.

He took the old marble staircase to the first floor, gripping the mahogany railing so his slick Italian loafers wouldn't slide out from under him. He nodded to the security guards and went outside, finding the air refreshing. Old government buildings were never the right temperature, too hot in the Winter or too cold in the Summer.

Damn the Senator. No one tells me how to vote. That man has been in DC too long. The power's gone to his head. Sterling's right. The bill can't pass.

He pulled out his cell phone and noticed his voicemail light flashing. There were two messages from Sterling, first one about being on the way to pick up Blythe. In the second message, Sterling began speaking, then stopped. He heard a man's voice in the background ordering her to hang up the phone, but the phone remained on. Smart girl. The voices were now further away from the phone, but Trevor heard Sterling's voice say, "Walker, please lower the gun. No one here is a threat to you," A muffled conversation

followed and BAM, a gunshot. The line went dead.

Oh my God. Walker shot someone! I've got to get over there.

If anyone's hurt, Walker will pay.

CHAPTER THIRTY

Walker hobbled out of Sterling's apartment, letting the door slam behind him. A couple of Sterling's neighbors peered into the hallway, but quickly retreated inside when they saw the crazed injured man.

Breathless, he leaned against the wall and wrapped his handkerchief around the wound on his leg, realizing the Escalade keys were in Vinnie's pocket.

Shit. Shit. Shit. I can't go back...

He headed for the Courthouse Metro stop. The five-minute walk took fifteen, with stops every few feet to wipe the sweat from his face and re-adjust his makeshift bandage. Once inside the station, Walker checked the schedule. The Union Station train would arrive in eight minutes. After a quick look around the platform, Walker turned his back to a snoring, inebriated man and called Sandy.

"Walker, where the fuck are you?" Sandy said.

"Shut up and listen to me. I may lose you. We have a situation, and we've got to get out of town for a while."

"What situation? What happened?"

"I'll tell you later, but Vinnie's dead."

"Holy shit. Where're we going?"

"Ok, listen to me. Don't say the town. Do you remember where I vacationed last Summer?"

"You mean…"

"I said keep your fucking mouth shut. Now, do you remember or not?"

"Yeah, yeah. I remember."

"Meet me there tonight. You need to leave within the hour."

"Sure."

"Don't call me."

"Ok. See you later."

"Make sure you're not followed."

CHAPTER THIRTY-ONE

From the back of a yellow cab, Trevor called the 911 and repeated what he heard transpire in Sterling's voicemail. He requested paramedics, police and a coroner.

He called Sterling on both her home and cell phones. No answer.

Hang on, Sterling.

The taxi pulled into the circle drive of Courtland Towers. Trevor tossed a $50 bill at the driver and raced out of the cab.

"Keep the change," he yelled over his shoulder.

I hope I'm not too late.

First thing he saw when exiting the elevator was a trail of blood leading to Sterling's door.

Oh my God.

He ran, calling "Sterling? Blythe? Tom? It's Trevor. Where are you?"

"Over here, Trevor, by the couch," Sterling said.

Relieved, he found Sterling sitting on the floor against the couch. She cradled Blythe in her lap, softly crying, and pressed a blood-soaked cloth against her sister's chest.

"Sterling. I got your voicemail. It cut off after the first gunshot. I didn't know if you were still alive. Are you ok? How's Blythe? Where's Tom?" He leaned over and gently kissed her on the cheek.

"Trevor, I'm sorry. Tom died trying to save us. A bullet hit my shoulder. I think it's still in there. It's not that bad. I'll be fine. I'm more concerned about Blythe. She needs a doctor."

"The paramedics and police are on their way. Let me see your shoulder."

Her shirt stuck to the wound.

"Can I get you anything for pain?"

"Some aspirin, please. There's some in the kitchen above the sink."

Trevor gagged when he saw the other bodies.

"Blythe's barely alive. I think she's in shock. I'm so glad you got my message. Vinnie cut the land line, then my cell phone died."

"Vinnie?" He said from the kitchen.

"That's him over there. He worked for Senator Morelli."

He gave her two aspirin with a glass of water.

"Senator Morelli's involved with this? But, why come here?"

He looked around Sterling's wrecked apartment.

"Walker and Sandy went to The Franklin to search my office. I saw Walker in the Archives and discovered he hid Harry's notes there. He left without seeing me, so I retrieved the notes. Then they saw me leave the building and Sandy chased me. I lost Sandy in the metro and escaped because of Tom's timely arrival."

"God bless Tom."

"When we got here, Walker and Vinnie were tearing my place apart. You know what all of this means, don't you? Harry's notes must prove that EMFs kill. We've got to stop Walker and Morelli. They'll do anything to get the Energy Bill passed."

Blythe stirred and grabbed Sterling's shirt, pulling her down.

"I've got to tell you something. My locket. Where's my locket?" Sterling lifted the blood-spattered necklace up so her sister could see it.

"Shh, Blythe your locket's right here. We can talk after we get you to the hospital." She put the locket in Blythe's hand.

"No, I need to tell you…"

They heard voices coming down the hallway. Paramedics barreled into the apartment.

"Over here, in the living room. These women have gunshot wounds and the two men on the floor are deceased," Trevor said as he nodded toward Tom and Vinnie.

The two male paramedics rolled the gurney close to Blythe.

"Ok, Miss, you can let go now," the first paramedic said.

"Please, help my sister. She can't die," Sterling said.

"We'll take care of her. Now, let me see your shoulder wound," the other paramedic said. "There's so much blood on you, I don't know which is yours and which is your sister's."

"I'll be fine. Please, just take care of my sister," Sterling said.

"OK. I'm going to clean your wound and give you some pain medicine," the paramedic said.

"No, no pain medicine. I already took aspirin."

"Suit yourself," the paramedic said as he cut open her shirt and put betadine on her wound. "The bullet is still in there, so you'll need to come with us to the hospital."

"Your sister's ready for transport. Hey, Joe, help me with the gurney."

"What's in the IV?" Sterling said.

An antibiotic and some pain medicine. It should help her rest until we get to the hospital." Blythe moaned as the paramedics placed her on the lowered stretcher.

"I'm riding with her in the ambulance," Sterling said.

"I'll follow you in my car. Which hospital?" Trevor asked.

"George Washington. It's the best for gunshot wounds."

As they rolled Blythe out into the hall, two men got off the elevator.

"Are you with the Arlington Police?" Trevor said.

"Yeah, I'm Detective Stan Hughes and this is my partner, Detective Doug Thomas," Detective Hughes said with his buzzed haircut and too-short tie.

"Detectives, I'm Congressman Reese. This is Sterling Barrington and her sister, Blythe Corbin, is on the gurney. They're heading to the hospital. You'll find two dead men in Ms. Barrington's apartment."

The paramedics rolled the gurney onto the elevator and Sterling stepped inside, leaning against the elevator door.

"Whoa. Wait up guys. I need to get a statement from these ladies," Detective Hughes said.

"Officer, please, my sister needs medical attention immediately. I'll fill you in on the way or even at the hospital, but I'm not leaving her side," Sterling said.

"Make a decision. We'll lose her if we don't get her to the hospital," the paramedic said.

"Dougie, you stay here with the Congressman and call forensics. I'll take Ms. Barrington's statement at the hospital."

"Works for me, Stan. Hey Congressman, can I hitch a ride with you to the ER?" Detective Thomas smoothed his trendy tie and ran a hand through his expensive haircut.

"Of course, Detective. Sterling, I'll be there as soon as I can," Trevor said.

"Detective Hughes, the shooters were Walker Nelson and Vinnie," Sterling managed to blurt out as the elevator doors closed.

CHAPTER THIRTY-TWO

The siren harshly echoed as the ambulance drove down into the underground ramp of George Washington University Hospital.

Four young doctors wearing scrubs and highly coveted white coats stood outside the emergency room entrance. The ambulance stopped and the doctors pounced on it like lions after prey. The paramedic who took care of Blythe jumped out first, handing his chart to the closest doctor. She took it and stepped aside as the other three pulled Blythe's gurney out.

"Hey, doc. This is Blythe Corbin. A forty-year-old, white female, with a GSW to the abdomen. She's lost a lot of blood. I gave her two units on the ride over so she's stable. This is the next of kin, her sister, Sterling Barrington. She's got a bullet in her right shoulder. I cleaned it up and bandaged it, but she turned down pain meds," the paramedic said as he helped Sterling out of the ambulance.

Detective Hughes walked up.

"Hello, detective. I'll answer your questions inside," said Sterling.

"Ok, let's get these two into the ER. I'm Dr. Wilhoit and I'll be taking care of Blythe. Dr. Bagby, take this one and check her shoulder," said Dr. Wilhoit gesturing toward Sterling.

"Thanks. Please, save her," Sterling said.

"Come with me, Ms. Barrington, is it?" Dr. Bagby said. He had a bed-head hairdo and five o'clock shadow, probably hadn't slept in days. He took Sterling's uninjured arm and led her to a wheelchair in the emergency room. "No, complaints. Hospital rules, so enjoy the ride."

Detective Hughes followed Dr. Bagby as he wheeled her around the noisy ER. Babies cried, couples argued, victims moaned. For Sterling it all ran rhythmically together like bees buzzing in a hive.

"Ms. Barrington, I need to question you now," Detective Hughes said.

"Detective, let me check her wound first."

"Ok, but make it fast."

The doctor turned into one of the curtained areas with beds where a female nurse waited. The nurse pulled the curtains around them and helped Sterling out of her ruined blouse into a hospital gown.

Dr. Bagby examined her wound. "Looks like the paramedics did a good job cleaning you up. I think the bullet cleared your collar bone, but let's get an x-ray just in case," he said.

After her x-ray, Sterling returned to the same curtained area. The bullet had indeed missed her collar bone. Dr. Bagby numbed her wounds, found and extracted the bullet, then stitched and bandaged her up.

"Here's some Tylenol for the pain you'll feel after the numbing agent wears off. We'll bag your clothes and this bullet for the cops."

"When will I hear something about my sister?"

"I'll find out."

A nurse helped Sterling to the waiting room and handed her a bag. "These are your sister's personal items," she said.

"Thank you."

Sterling looked in the bag. Blythe's watch and locket were inside.

Detective Hughes came over to her.

"Ms. Barrington, can I get your statement about this evening's events," Detective Hughes asked.

"Sure," Sterling said, taking a deep breath. "But I'll need to go back a few days to give you the full picture."

She told him about Walker and why he came to her apartment with Vinnie. She also recounted what she knew about Harry and that she believed Walker killed him to conceal industry secrets.

"You might want to contact the Baltimore detectives, Keegan and Angelo. They're investigating Harry's murder."

A nurse approached and handed Hughes a bag, "Excuse me Detective, here are the victims' clothes and the bullet pulled from Ms. Barrington."

"Thanks. I'll be in touch, Ms. Barrington. Here's my card if you think of anything else."

"There you are," Trevor and Detective Thomas walked up to them.

"You done with Ms. Barrington, Stan?" Detective Thomas said.

"Yeah, we can head out."

"Thank you, Detectives."

The two men left, and Trevor put his arm around Sterling. She winced. "Oh, sorry! Are you in a lot of pain?"

"I'll be fine, but Blythe's in surgery and I haven't heard anything since they took her in."

They drank bad coffee and flipped through out-of-date magazines to pass the time. After a couple of hours, Dr. Wilhoit walked up, pulling a surgical mask down to her neck.

"Ms. Barrington, your sister's out of surgery. It's going to be touch and go for a while."

"Thank you, doctor. When can I see her?"

"You can come back to recovery now. She'll be awake soon."

"I'll wait here, Sterling," Trevor said.

Sterling followed Dr. Wilhoit to the low-lit recovery room, which smelled strongly of bleach and antiseptic. Nurses tended to patients behind curtained walls. The doctor stepped up to a bed near the back wall.

"How are her vitals? She said to one of the nurses nearby as she checked Blythe's IV line.

"They're the same," the nurse said.

Dr. Wilhoit motioned to a chair by the bed, "You can sit here Ms. Barrington. They'll move her to a room once she's stable."

Sterling moved the chair closer to Blythe's bed and placed a hand over her sister's.

"Um, where am I?" Blythe said.

"You're in the hospital, Blythe. You were shot."

"I remember now."

You just came out of surgery. You're going to be fine."

"Sterling, I have to tell you something. Where's my locket?"

"It's right here with your other things."

"Let me see it. Now, please."

"Here it is," Sterling handed her the golden necklace.

Blythe draped the chain around her hand and caressed the locket.

She whispered, "Sterling. I've kept a secret, a secret that caused us to get hurt tonight."

Sterling leaned closer to her sister, "What are you talking about?"

"I have Harry's notes."

"You have Harry's notes?"

"Yes. I found them at Harry's. In the bag of dry cat food. I know it sounds crazy. When I found Harry dead and the house trashed, I thought his killer took them. I…I…I haven't seen a dead body since…well, you know, and needed to calm my nerves so I went to the kitchen for some water. Then I saw the cat, now your cat. The poor thing was in shock, so I found some cat food. I looked inside the bag for a scoop but unearthed a sealed plastic container instead. In it were Harry's disks. I'm so sorry. I should have told you that night."

"Blythe, where are they?"

"I hid them in a locker in the Vienna metro station. The key's inside my locket. Take it and get his notes. For Christopher and the other innocent victims."

"If you have Harry's notes, then I must have Walker's. He thought I took Harry's notes, so he doesn't know I have his evidence."

"I'm scared Sterling. What if he comes after us again?"

"He's on the run, now. We don't have to worry about him, and now we have all the evidence we need to prove that EMFs kill."

"Harry wanted the truth to be made public. I know you will respect his wishes." Blythe's lashes fluttered and she sighed deeply.

"Of course, Blythe. We'll get the truth out together."

"No, Sterling. I'm tired. I miss Christopher."

"Blythe, don't say that. I need you. Please."

Blythe's eyes closed and the locket she'd been holding fell to the floor.

Panicked, Sterling cried out, "Nurse, I need help here."

A nurse came over, checked Blythe's pulse and IV.

"Miss, you need to leave now. I'm paging the doctor."

Sterling retrieved the locket from the floor and pleaded with her sister, "No, wait. Blythe, I love you. You can't leave me again."

Very quietly, Blythe said, "Christopher. I'm here, my angel."

CHAPTER THIRTY-THREE

The two Arlington detectives walked out of the George Washington Hospital emergency room.

"Ms. Barrington told me Walker Nelson looks good for murdering some guy named Harry Brown in Baltimore. She gave me the name of the officers on that case. Let's give them a call and compare notes," Detective Hughes said.

"Works for me."

Detective Hughes pulled out his notepad and dialed a number on his cell phone.

"Baltimore Police," a female voice said.

"I need to speak with Detective Keegan in Homicide."

"One moment, please."

"Keegan, homicide."

"Hello, this is Detective Hughes of the Arlington PD. We're working on a case that may tie in with one of yours."

"Which one?"

"The Harry Brown murder. We had a shooting this evening with two dead and two wounded. One of the wounded told me to call you."

"Sheesh, sounds like a bloodbath. Who gave you my name?"

"Ms. Sterling Barrington."

"Crap. Did Ms. Barrington know the shooter?"

"Yes, she said Walker Nelson and Vinnie Tirello were responsible. They took Ms. Barrington, her sister and an older guy, Tom Whitaker, hostage at her apartment. Whitaker and Tirello are dead, Nelson's in the wind."

"What a mess. Tell me about the sister?"

"Blythe Corbin took a round to the gut. She's in surgery at George Washington."

"I actually arrested Ms. Barrington today for being an accomplice to Brown's murder."

"Evidence?"

"Yeah, we found DNA of a Barrington sibling at the Brown scene. Figured she must be an accessory or just covering for the relative."

"So, you think the sister murdered Brown? Ms. Barrington accused her boss, Walker Nelson, of the murder. Says he was trying to cover up industry secrets."

"We didn't find his prints or DNA at the crime scene, but we did find some other DNA at Brown's house, from a guy named Sandford Matthews. Why don't you meet us at his condo on Sixth and Penn?"

"Sure, we're not far. What's the unit number?"

"It's unit 430. Oh yeah, this Matthews guy is also linked to another murder in DC so be careful."

"Thanks for the tip."

"And thank you for the head's up about Nelson. We'll put out an APB out on him. See you in a few."

CHAPTER THIRTY-FOUR

Sterling walked out of the recovery room clutching Blythe's locket to her chest and wiping away tears. Trevor rushed over and hugged her.

"She's gone, Trevor. She's gone."

"Sterling, I'm so sorry."

"She's with Christopher now."

"I wish you had more time with her."

"Yes, so do I," Sterling pulled away from Trevor. "Right now though, we need to leave. I promised Blythe I'd do something for her."

"Now? What is it?"

Sterling looked around the room and leaned in to Trevor, "Not here."

Once in the car, Trevor said, "Okay, we're safely stowed away, where to?"

"The Vienna Metro Station."

"Why? What's there?"

"Harry's notes."

CHAPTER THIRTY-FIVE

Sandy stood outside his apartment, mentally checking items off his to-do list. Suitcase packed, check. Trash taken out, check. Lights off, check. Extra cash, check. Satisfied he'd covered everything, he started to lock his door.

"Sandy Matthews? Stop right there. Arlington Police," a deep male voice said from down the hall.

Sandy stopped and looked at the two men in suits, guns unholstered, walking toward him. He dropped his keys and ran to the emergency exit.

"FREEZE! Sandy Matthews, you're under arrest for the murder of Bob Turner," one of the detectives said.

The other detective grabbed Sandy's arm, slammed him up against the wall and handcuffed him. At that moment, Detectives Keegan and Angelo walked off the elevator.

"Is this our guy?" Keegan said.

"Yes. Detectives, meet Sandford 'Sandy' Matthews. He's been a busy boy. Haven't you Sandy? Let me introduce everyone here. We're Detective Hughes and Thomas from the Arlington police.

We need to ask some questions about your boss, Walker Nelson. And these are some of Baltimore's finest, Detectives Keegan and Angelo. They want to ask you about the murder of Harry Brown."

"I have nothing to say to any of you," Sandy said.

"Oh yeah? What's with the suitcase? Leaving town? Guilty conscience?"

"Just a business trip. I've got nothing to hide."

"Yeah, yeah. I've never heard that before. Thomas, read him his rights so we can get the party started at headquarters."

CHAPTER THIRTY-SIX

Walker took a train from Union Station to Rehoboth Beach, Delaware. There were about ten passengers who exited at stops along the route, leaving him alone for the last hour of the journey.

His injured leg throbbed. He wanted a cigarette badly, but this train was rigged with smoke detectors.

Shit. I need a distraction, anything, so I can stop focusing on the fucking pain.

He eyed his duffel bag.

Hmmmmm. Maybe I brought...oh God please.

Walker rifled through his duffle bag, tossing socks here and shirts there. A smile spread across his face when a bottle of vodka emerged. He downed half its contents.

What a fucking day. And I still don't have Harry's notes. It's all his fault. If he hadn't given his notes to Sterling, I wouldn't be in this mess. I hope that bitch bled out.

He gulped down more vodka.

Morelli and his mobsters are probably already after me, payback for Vinnie's death. Sandy and I will figure out next steps once he gets to the beach house.

Walker finished the vodka and dozed off, waking when the conductor announced, "Rehoboth Beach, exit at the front of the car."

Known as the Nation's Summer Capital, this seaside resort overflowed with DC residents in the warm months. Walker only came for the free lodging at his in-law's beach house.

As the empty train pulled out of the station, he threw his bag down and lit a cigarette. He took a few puffs then flicked the butt away. He hobbled across to the nearly empty long-term parking, where his in-laws left their SUV. He opened the door, sat down, and gingerly pulled his wounded leg into the Trailblazer. He moaned and bit his lip.

Shit.

He needed more to drink or a powerful pain killer. Or both. Luckily, he kept a stash at the house. The town was in hibernation mode until the summer so there was zero traffic. Lucky for him, since he was trying to drive with his left foot.

At long last, Walker pulled into a gravel driveway. It took him at least 5 sweaty minutes to move his leg and get out of the SUV. He limped to the front door and retrieved a house key from under the welcome mat. Blood was running down his leg.

After getting the car in the garage, he went inside the house. Built in the 1960's, it still had the original, vintage furniture and accessories. His in-laws didn't like change.

Everything was dusty. Walker opened a few windows to clear the air. He took off his coat and tie, draped them over a sheet-covered couch and went to the bookshelf. Opening Thomas Edison's biography revealed a flask of vodka and bottle of Vicodin. He took a swig from the flask and swallowed four pills.

That'll help.

He took a shower, dressed his wound and iced it down with a bag of frozen corn.

Sandy should be here soon.

He picked up his cell phone and dialed Sandy's cell. It went straight to voicemail.

Where the fuck is he?

He put some throw pillows under his foot and leaned back on the couch.

I'll go to Canada. That's what I'll do.

He took another swallow of Vodka and drifted off.

CHAPTER THIRTY-SEVEN

"I can still smell Tom's cologne in here," Sterling said, heavily sighing. "I called his family and told them I'd pay for the funeral arrangements."

"Do you want me to put that bag in the trunk for you?" Trevor asked.

"No. I want to hold it. It's all I have left of Blythe."

"So, how did Blythe get Harry's notes?"

"The cat told her."

"What?"

"When she arrived at Harry's, she found him dead, the house torn apart. She presumed the killer took Harry's evidence. Then the cat, Raven, wandered into the living room and laid on Harry's feet. Blythe felt bad for Raven and wanted to comfort her, so she started searching for food. She found a bag in the kitchen and, when she poured it into a bowl, a baggie with disks fell out.

"I can't believe she had Harry's evidence all this time. I'm glad she finally realized she could trust you and tell you about it."

"Yes, and we'll honor her memory by making Harry's and Walker's notes public and stopping that energy bill."

"Good plan. Here we are, the Vienna metro station."

Sterling leaned against Trevor as they walked inside and squeezed Blythe's locket for luck. As they approached the luggage lockers, Sterling opened the locket and took out a key.

"We need to find number 220."

"Over there."

The locker held the baggie with disks they had just discussed and two letters, one addressed to Sterling and the other to Carter.

"Do you want to read her letter?" Carter asked when they were back in the car.

"No, not yet."

"Are you going to send that letter to Carter?"

"Yes, she wanted him to have it."

"Let's get you back home."

"Trevor, after we go through Harry's and Walker's notes, will you call for an emergency hearing of the energy committee?"

"Yes. I'll send the announcement out tonight. Thanks to your tape recorder, I've also got a recording of my meeting with Morelli. I'll make a copy and send it to the police for their investigation."

Sterling put Blythe's locket around her neck and kissed it. Christopher and Blythe's deaths would not be in vain.

CHAPTER THIRTY-EIGHT

Back at the SAFEPOWER compound, Carter's team was buzzing about the rally's success. Carter was in no mood to celebrate.

Why wouldn't Blythe answer her phone?

He hadn't informed the Speaker yet about her kidnapping.

Victim or traitor? Did Blythe go with Sterling voluntarily?

For the first time in his life, he had let himself care about someone. He thought she felt the same way. He even planned to propose to her after the rally. He wanted her to always be by his side, fighting the good fight against the evil empires of the world.

Would he ever see her again?

His muted television, tuned to CNN, showed a clip from their rally. He turned up the volume and heard a relatively positive report about SAFEPOWER. The next segment was about an Arlington shooting involving multiple victims. Carter reached for the remote and had his finger hovering over the OFF button when he heard the anchor say:

"Police have confirmed the identity of two victims: Sterling Barrington of The Franklin Electric Institute and her sister Blythe Corbin of the environmental group, SAFEPOWER."

Blythe's been shot?

The reporter continued with the facts. The two women were held hostage and wounded. Two other men were shot and killed. Their names would not be released until families had been notified. The alleged shooter, a Mr. Walker Nelson of DC, was the prime suspect and had not yet been apprehended by police. Walker's driver license photo appeared on the screen behind the anchor.

Nelson shot them? He's in cahoots with Senator Morelli on the energy bill. Did Morelli order a hit?

Breaking news flashed on the screen and the anchor continued,

"This just in from the field. It appears Ms. Corbin died of her gunshot wounds at George Washington Hospital. The Arlington Police encourage viewers to call with any information about Walker Nelson and this now triple homicide."

Dead? Blythe's gone?

Carter called the Speaker. It went straight to voicemail.

Damn. Probably with his latest mistress.

He left a detailed message of the evening's events and ended by saying he would get revenge against The Franklin for Blythe's death.

He hung up the phone and looked into the great room. The rest of the team members were asleep. He closed his office door and locked it. From the top shelf of a closet, he pulled out an aluminum briefcase.

Carter took a deep breath and opened it. Inside, a green military-style vest with multiple pockets. Each pocket contained an explosive. He caressed each one.

The Speaker gave it to him a few years before as a last resort in their war against the electric industry. He never questioned how the Speaker acquired the vest. Men with that level of wealth could get whatever they wanted.

Carter left the safe house with the briefcase. Killing Blythe was the final insult.

CHAPTER THIRTY-NINE

Detective Hughes pushed a sweaty, huffing Sandy into the back seat of his unmarked sedan.

"Guess you should hit the gym more often if you plan to outrun cops," Hughes said.

Sandy ignored him, squirming uncomfortably in the seat thanks to the handcuffs.

On the drive to the police station, Detective Thomas called his girlfriend, who worked at one of the network television affiliates, and gave her the scoop on Sandy. Wouldn't take long for the press hounds to take the bait.

"You ready to be famous for all the wrong reasons, Matthews?" Thomas asked.

The sedan stopped in front of the police station and was immediately bombarded by flashing cameras.

"Oh shit," Sandy said

"Yeah, pretty boy, this is all for you. The world needs to know what evil looks like," Detective Hughes said.

The detectives pulled Sandy out of the car.

"Mr. Matthews, is it true you murdered two people? Are you a serial killer?" A pretty reporter asked.

"No comment," Sandy said.

"But our citizens need to know. Why did you commit these heinous acts?"

"I said no fucking comment."

"Hey, watch your mouth, Matthews. Treat the lady with respect," Detective Thomas winked at her.

After the media circus got their fill, Detective Hughes dumped Sandy in an interrogation room and handcuffed him to the table.

"Is this really necessary? I can't go anywhere."

"And whose fault is that?" Detective Hughes said, leaving the room.

Both the Arlington and Baltimore detectives looked at Sandy through the two-way glass. "Who wants to start the questioning?" Detective Angelo inquired.

"I guess we'll go first and question him about Bob Turner. Then, you two can grill him about your case. Remind me the guy's name," Detective Thomas said.

"Brown, Harry Brown" Detective Keegan said.

"Alright, then. Some housekeeping tips, the vending machine and coffee pot are around the corner, the heads at the end of the hall. It's going to be a long night, gang. I'll have the department assistant order us some pizzas."

CHAPTER FORTY

"Why did you murder Bob Turner? Not a good lay? Is that why you fried him up like a KFC drumstick?" Detective Thomas said.

"I didn't kill him, and I'm not gay. I never even went to his apartment," said Sandy angrily.

"That's interesting. We didn't tell you where he died. I guess you know because you were there. In his bed."

"What? No, um. I've never been anywhere near his bed."

"Mr. Matthews, tell us what happened. We can help you," Hughes said.

"Ok, I went to his apartment. We talked about work, that's all."

"So, after you killed him, you wiped down everything in the apartment, but you missed something. We found your prints on Mr. Turner's body and on the murder weapon, the stereo," Thomas said.

"I don't know how my fingerprints got on him."

"Well, I know how they did. Sex. And you forgot to wipe down the stereo cord after you removed it from the tub."

"No, nothing happened."

"Just so happens we have your prints on file, back from when you beat your wife. And you'll never guess! They match the prints found on the corpse. You're a real lowlife aren't you, Matthews?"

"Ex-wife. And I only hit her once."

"Only once. Thomas, quit giving this guy such a hard time," Hughes said.

"Yeah, he's a real sweetheart, this one. So, when did your ex find out you like boys? That'll make you real popular in prison."

"I told you, I'm not gay."

"Keep telling yourself that, Matthews. We're done here. Next up, Baltimore."

"Mr. Matthews, to refresh your memory, I'm Detective Keegan and this is Detective Angelo. So, tell us why you killed Harry Brown?"

"I didn't."

"Yeah, you did, and we have a witness."

"A witness? Who?"

"It's more of a what than a who."

"What do you mean?"

"I mean we know Brown's cat scratched you. Probably there, on your ear where you've got a bandage. We found your DNA lodged in the cat's paw."

"That's ridiculous! No jury will believe it."

"We have a world-renowned forensics department that can prove it."

"Shit, that damn cat."

"Now, why don't you tell us what happened? Why did you murder an old, helpless guy?" Detective Angelo said.

"Not my idea. I followed orders, from Morelli."

"Morelli? Senator Morelli? The big wig on the hill? Why did he want Brown whacked?" Keegan said.

"He needs the energy bill passed or his constituents won't vote for him again. He found out Brown threatened to release information that would hurt the industry. If his papers became public, and the bill didn't pass, our careers were over. I didn't mean to kill Brown. He just wouldn't help us."

"You're saying, Harry died due to an accident?"

"Yeah, an accident."

"Cords don't just wrap themselves around people's neck."

"Maybe he offed himself. I'm not a killer. I went to talk to him. That's it."

"You're not a killer? I think the Arlington detectives would disagree with you."

"Oh man, my life's falling apart."

"So, help yourself and tell us about Morelli's involvement. Maybe the DA can cut you a deal."

"A deal? What kind of deal?"

"No deal until we hear what you know about Morelli and how Walker Nelson fits in with this mess?" Detective Angelo said.

"Nelson's my boss. He had nothing to do with this. We both reported to Morelli."

"Where's Nelson now?" Keegan said.

"I don't know."

"So, where were you going when you were arrested? To meet Walker? Looked like you packed for a long trip," Angelo said.

"No real place in mind, I just wanted to get out of town."

"We pulled your phone records. Walker called you this evening from his cell phone...right after he shot two women. We'll have his location soon. Do you happen to know why Walker was at Sterling Barrington's apartment?"

"Walker is no killer, but that Barrington is a real sneaky bitch. He was probably there looking for Harry's notes, which she stole."

"We're done for now. We may have more questions after you're booked."

"Wait, what about my deal? Are you going to talk to the DA in Baltimore?"

"You write down everything you know about Morelli's involvement in Brown's murder, and we'll take it to the DA. I'm not making any promises."

All four detectives mulled over Sandy's confession while eating pizza.

"So, let's regroup. We know Matthews killed Brown and Turner. Considering he's Nelson's errand boy, he must know where he is," Hughes said.

"Yeah, he must be too afraid of Nelson to talk. So, we'll take him with us to Baltimore and get him arraigned for Brown's murder, then bring him back to DC for the Turner murder," Keegan said.

"That doesn't work for us. We collared the guy," Thomas said and nodded to Hughes.

"Guys, we all want this scumbag to go down. Hughes and Thomas, you can arraign him today, and we'll take him to Baltimore in a couple of days," Angelo said.

"Ok. We'll have him ready for you."

"Glad that's settled. New business, we need to widen our search area for Nelson and figure out how Senator Morelli is involved," Hughes said.

"Hang on, team. Let me get this call from GW," Detective Thomas said and motioned to the group to be quiet. "Thomas, here. Yes, ok, thanks for the call," He closed his phone and said. "We need to add another victim to the Nelson hit list. Blythe Corbin died."

"Shit. Poor Ms. Corbin. She died protecting her sister," Angelo said.

"Well, let's get this S.O.B. then. We owe her," Keegan said.

CHAPTER FORTY-ONE

The Navy Memorial fountains splashed melodically as Carter walked to the middle of the plaza and opened the briefcase. His cell phone rang.

"Carter, what's going on? What do you mean revenge?" the Speaker said.

"I'm taking care of it. The electric industry killed one too many tonight."

"Where are you?"

"I'm in front of The Franklin."

"Carter, after what happened tonight, the bill won't pass. We won. You won."

"No, they killed Blythe and deserve to be punished."

"What do you mean, they killed Blythe?"

"Walker Nelson killed her because he was trying to hide the damage his industry has done."

"Nelson killed Blythe? Let the police handle this."

"An eye for an eye."

Carter, this is a mistake. It's extreme, and I won't be linked to this level of violence."

"You said the murderers must be stopped. That their killings must end. I'm going to ensure that happens."

"Not this way."

"Goodbye, Mr. Speaker."

Carter dropped his phone in the fountain and walked to The Franklin's front entrance. He held the detonator in his right hand.

"I love you, Blythe."

CHAPTER FORTY-TWO

Walker's ankle ached, and his head pounded. The pillows were wet from the melted corn bag, which had fallen to the floor.

Where am I? What the fuck?

He looked at his wound. The ice had reduced the swelling, but the area around the wound had turned an angry red, making Blythe's bite marks more pronounced. It was probably infected.

He picked up his cell phone from the coffee table. *Fuck.* It was nearly dead, and he'd forgotten a charger. There were five messages from Eileen, but none from Sandy.

Eileen's voicemails started calm but ended panicky. "Where did he go? Why hadn't he called? The police came to question her, about a murder. What did he do?"

She can wait.

Walker pulled a new bottle of vodka out of the liquor cabinet and drank a quarter of it. *Sandy should be here by now.*

He called him and again got voicemail.

Shit. Shit. Shit. What's he doing?

He threw the phone down on the counter and heard his stomach growl. He rummaged through the freezer and found a box of toaster waffles. He brushed off the ice crystals and put two in the toaster oven. It dinged done and he took his food into the den.

Walker was skipping through TV channels when something caught his eye, a shot of The Franklin building on fire. The news channel reported that The Franklin Energy Institute in Washington, DC, had been attacked by the leader of SAFEPOWER environmental group.

Numerous fire, police and EMS vehicles surrounded the plaza. Walker rubbed his eyes and turned up the volume.

SAFEPOWER blew up The Franklin?

The reporter continued, "Authorities claim the blast only involved one fatality, the perpetrator, Carter Simpson."

The building's front had collapsed, but the structural engineers called to the scene, believed the rest of the building could be saved.

I can't believe those wackos did this. At least that lunatic Simpson was dead. Maybe that's why Sandy's not here yet. He probably couldn't get through that mess since he lives across the street.

Walker flipped through more channels, landing on CSPAN.

"We're on the hill awaiting the start of an emergency meeting of the joint Energy Committee. Congressman Trevor Reese, Democrat from Atlanta, called this meeting, but the reason for its urgency hasn't been released. This committee's Energy Bill was scheduled to go to vote next week. This meeting may change the course of that bill," the blonde reporter said.

Shit. What's this crap? I hope Morelli has this under control. What's Reese got planned?

"As we pan around the hearing room, we see the committee members taking their seats. Senator Morelli, Chairman of this joint committee, just entered the room. Our sources tell us the redheaded woman on the front row, wearing a sling, is the key witness in today's meeting," the reporter continued. The camera zoomed in for a closeup. Sterling sat in the front row.

She's alive? Damn it all to hell.

"I just got word that Baltimore police are in the hearing room to arrest Senator Morelli on murder charges. It appears a female detective has read the Senator his rights and put him in handcuffs. One of our field reporters is getting more information about the arrest.

This emergency hearing hasn't begun yet, but it's already full of surprises. Let's listen as Congressman Reese calls the meeting to order."

Walker grabbed the vodka, the car keys, and ran out of the house. He pulled out of the driveway and headed north.

CHAPTER FORTY-THREE

"Ms. Barrington, thank you for testifying today. We realize how much courage it takes to come forward after the tragedy you've recently faced. Please tell me more about the link between power lines, EMFs, and the EHS illness," said Congresswoman Athena Winter of Maine.

"Congresswoman Winter, according to Walker Nelson's and Harry Brown's notes, studies performed by the DOE and the UK's RAS confirm that power lines, transmission towers and substations emit EMFs. The research further states that when electric transmitting facilities are in close proximity to humans, there is a documented increase in illnesses and deaths."

The audience murmured amongst themselves, and reporters typed furiously on their Blackberries, sending the updated information to their television stations, newspapers and blogs.

"I said order. No more talking and no more use of electronic devices. You will be escorted out. Next, Congressman Batch of Utah, go ahead with your questions," Trevor said.

The committee members continued to question Sterling and the audience remained silent during the rest of the hearing.

"We will take a 30-minute recess for the committee to discuss these findings. Please exit the room. Ms. Barrington will not be answering questions from the press corps at this time," Trevor said.

The same two Capitol Hill police, who escorted Sterling into the room, escorted her to an unmarked office.

"Ms. Barrington, would you like any coffee or water?" one of the officers asked.

"Coffee would be great, thanks. Cream, no sugar."

The door closed behind her and the other officer stood outside to keep unwanted visitors away.

Sterling walked over to the window. Even with the security wire between the panes, the view of the Capitol was unobscured, and the flag on top waved in the breeze.

The officer brought her the coffee.

"If you need anything else, I'll be in the next room. We'll come get you when it's time to go back to the hearing room."

"Thank you, officer."

She sipped her coffee and rolled her neck. She had a knot in her stomach and her shoulders ached.

Did I do enough to stop the bill? I can't bring Christopher, Harry or Blythe back, but their senseless deaths need to be vindicated.

"They're ready for you, Ms. Barrington."

"The Committee appreciates the honest testimony of Ms. Sterling Barrington and has unanimously voted to cancel the Energy Bill. Furthermore, the Committee would like Ms. Barrington to chair a power transmission taskforce to find safer, more efficient energy distribution methods. This bipartisan taskforce will use Harry Brown's and Walker Nelson's original research as a starting point. Ms. Barrington, we ask that you provide monthly reports to this joint committee. Once the taskforce completes its research and shares its findings, a new Energy Bill will be proposed."

"Congressman Reese, I accept this position and will, to the best of my abilities, find a safer, more efficient method of transmitting electricity."

"I hereby close this emergency meeting of the Joint House/Senate Energy Committee," Trevor said.

CHAPTER FORTY-FOUR

Sterling slipped her hand into Trevor's when the soldier started playing Taps. They were at Arlington National Cemetery for Tom Whitaker's funeral. The minister finished his homilies and asked Trevor to come forward.

"I had the privilege of working with Tom every day. Tom was a hero in war and a hero in life. In his honor, I have established the Tom Whitaker foundation to help the victims of EMFs. Tom will be missed."

A twenty-one-gun salute started, and guests placed red roses on Tom's casket. A fitting tribute to the man who died trying to save Sterling and Blythe.

After saying their goodbyes to Tom's loved ones, Sterling and Trevor walked arm in arm through the maze of stark white crosses.

"Now I have to plan Blythe's service," Sterling reached into her purse and turned on her cellphone. She had a voicemail from Detective Thomas of the Arlington police.

"More police questions. I'll call him now."

"I'll drive us back to your place."

"Detective Thomas, this is Sterling Barrington. How may I help you?"

"Ms. Barrington, thanks for returning my call. I got your number from Keegan in Baltimore. I need to ask you about Carter Thompson."

"I only met the man once. He brainwashed my sister and convinced her to join SAFEPOWER. Then he blew up my former place of work, The Franklin."

"That's what I'm calling about. The bomb squad said his explosives were old, which saved the rest of the building and, potentially, prevented casualties. Did you or your sister know of any plans to bomb The Franklin?"

"No. Maybe when he heard about my sister's death, he went over the edge."

"We're still looking for the SAFEPOWER headquarters. Did your sister tell you about it?"

"No, she never mentioned it. But my sister did leave me some items in a locker at the Vienna Metro Station. Maybe she picked that spot because it's close to their headquarters."

"Thanks, that helps. We'll move our search to that area."

"Good luck, Detective. Keep me posted."

CHAPTER FORTY-FIVE

Sterling had Blythe buried next to Christopher in Atlanta. During the funeral, peach trees and blooming azaleas swayed in the balmy breeze. She smiled and stroked Blythe's locket, which she always carried.

Mother and son, together forever.

Sterling flew back to DC. Trevor was waiting at the airport with a dozen red roses and much-needed hug.

"Let's get out of town for a few days, something fun," Trevor whispered in her ear.

"That would be wonderful. Let's talk about it tomorrow."

"Great."

He dropped her at the apartment building, which was no longer a crime scene. He couldn't understand why she wanted to stay in a place haunted by so much death.

Raven waited by the door as Sterling walked inside. She laid her purse and suitcase down, and scooped up the cat, holding her close.

"Hi Raven. Did you miss me?"

The cat nuzzled her and purred. She put her down and opened a can of cat food.

Sterling unpacked, checked her voicemail, and went through her mail – magazines, coupons, bills. It was nice to do routine tasks again. A plain envelope with no return address, postmarked Rehoboth Beach, DE, caught her attention. She tore open the envelope and pulled out a single piece of paper.

"It's not over, Sterling."

ABOUT THE AUTHOR

Jana Laird Phillips is a native Texan, who has lived and worked in Dallas, Washington DC and Houston. She is a BBA graduate of Baylor University with a double major in Marketing and Journalism. Ms. Phillips worked in the Energy Industry for several years, and has numerous articles published in Energy trade journals. She is currently the publisher/owner of an online magazine, HoustonHipandHaute.com.

Find out more at JanaLairdPhillips.com